P9-CFV-766

The Cellar

Ken Radford

The Cellar

Holiday House / New York

Library of Congress Cataloging-in-Publication Data

Radford, Ken.
    The cellar / written by Ken Radford.—1st ed.
        p.   cm.
    Summary: From her first night in an old boarding house located in
the hills of North Wales, a young girl is aware of mysterious
ghostly presences and determines to find an explanation for the
haunting.
    ISBN 0-8234-0744-6
    [1. Ghosts—Fiction.   2. Wales—Fiction.]   I. Title.
PZ7.R117Ce   1989
[Fic]—dc19   88-24708   CIP   AC

ISBN 0-8234-0744-6

For LAUREN *and* ELYSIA

Contents

The Cellar

CHAPTER 1

Cradle of the Winds

It was late in the afternoon one November day when Siân first set eyes on Crud-yr-Awel. Beyond a pathway fringed with conifers she glimpsed its walls standing black against the darkening sky. No lights glowed in the windows. The house was silent, menacing, like a thundercloud hovering on the horizon.

"This is the place," said the cabdriver, drawing to the side of the road. "Crud-yr-Awel—Cradle of the Winds. There are rarely any visitors at this time of the year."

He shone a flashlight toward the gate, its rays flickering silver and green among the trees. Then he opened the door for his passenger to alight and laid her traveling bag on the curb beside her.

"A bleak old house," he observed, glancing over his shoulder. "Dreary as a tomb."

While Siân fumbled in her purse his flashlight shone upon her flaxen hair, falling awry over her forehead.

"If you are afraid of the dark I'll walk along the path with you," he suggested with a mischievous grin.

3

"There's nothing to fear," Siân smiled. "I shall be all right, thank you."

For one so young she was well able to fend for herself. The survivor of a broken home and a fugitive from uncaring foster parents, there was little to learn of loneliness and times of despair that fortune had to offer.

For as long as she could remember she had been alone. Through childhood and school days, lying awake in the quiet of her room, even in the hustle and flurry of the city streets. Alone—always alone.

She stood at the roadside until the lights of the cab grew faint in the distance. Then she slung the traveling bag from her shoulder and approached the gateway to Crud-yr-Awel.

A low wall surrounded the garden, warped and crumbling with neglect. Threading her way along the path, she watched the evergreens tremble and sway, sometimes stretching out their fingers to touch her as she passed.

Her long years of solitude had kindled an imagination that raged wild as a forest fire. But here in the dusky light of evening she was not too afraid, for someone known to her as Faraway was a constant companion, always there to whisper words of comfort or cry out a warning of danger.

Faraway, her phantom friend, existed only in her imagination, but had stayed with her through moments of happiness and all those times of fear and misgiving. It was long ago when he came to her in a dream and lingered on. He grew no older with the passing years. And although no other knew his lilting voice and eyes as bright as dewdrops, Siân could conjure his presence whenever she wished. Perhaps it was because he came from some distant place, some unknown time, that she gave him such a strange name.

He was waiting at her bedside when she awoke early that morning, watched her gather her few belongings and steal down the stairs, gasped as she took from the bureau drawer money that was rightfully hers, sat with her in the railway compartment while they journeyed from the city. Even now he held her hand as they wandered along toward the shadowy porch.

"It looks so eerie," Faraway seemed to whisper, softly as a sigh of the wind. "Don't go any farther!"

Icy fingers clutched more tightly and drew her back.

"That's only because it's cold and dark," murmured Siân. "When dawn shows and the rays of sunlight come slanting through the trees, the shadows will melt away. You'll see. There's nothing to fear."

After a few moments of hesitation she rattled on the knocker, and the sound of it echoed in the hallway beyond the door.

"I'm afraid . . . I'm afraid!" breathed Faraway, tugging at her sleeve. But Siân knocked again.

Presently a light appeared at the window above the door. And when she turned around, her make-believe companion backed away and vanished in the darkness.

A key turned in the lock and the door creaked open, wide enough for a face to peer out.

"I'm . . . I'm Siân," the visitor stammered, searching for a letter in her pocket. "You asked that I come . . . Sorry to be so late . . . When I left the station I lost my way and then . . ."

The door opened wider, and a woman stood at the

threshold. Siân held forward the crumpled letter she had found.

For a while the woman stood there, clutching a shawl about her neck and looking a little bewildered.

"Miss Emily wrote asking that I come," Siân ventured.

"Well now, my goodness," smiled the mistress of Crud-yr-Awel. "What a pleasant surprise. Won't you come in from the cold?"

She took Siân's arm and shut out the early chill of winter. Then she called to someone who was watching from the far end of the hallway. "It's our new companion, Frances dear. She has traveled all the way from the city, and on such a miserable day."

She led Siân along the bare stone floor, reluctant to release her hold on their visitor's arm. "And as pretty a young lady as ever you did see."

Together they made their way to a spacious room at the rear of the house, where a log fire burned in the grate and a grandfather clock solemnly measured each passing moment.

From the wall hung an array of pictures in heavy gilt frames, each portraying a nautical scene—majestic liners steaming along the ocean, galleons with guns ablaze, sailing vessels tossed by wind and wave. Siân stared around in wonder, for she had never seen a room so long and tall, with the far corners plunged in thunderous shadow.

"Come, warm yourself by the fire," invited Miss Emily. "You must be cold and exhausted after your journey."

On the other side of the hearth sat the sisters, Frances

and Emily. From their manner and appearance no one would have realized they were closely related, for while Emily was fair with a pleasant smile, Frances wore a dark frown and her sharp eyes glittered in the firelight.

"We wondered whether you would come," said Frances, looking at Siân suspiciously. "We thought the dark walls and the murmuring wind of Crud-yr-Awel had frightened you away. It's happened before," she remembered, turning to her sister with a scowl.

Emily shrugged helplessly. "It's true," she sighed. "Others have come and gone. Perhaps the house is too quiet and far away for some."

"And the nights are dark and long," her sister added bitterly.

"We shall do all we can to make you happy here," Emily promised. "Then perhaps you will stay longer."

With nowhere else to go, there was little fear of Siân running away. There were no parents with whom she could share her troubles, no friends, no relatives. She had found no comfort or affection at her foster home, and would roam the city streets rather than return there. So, despite Faraway's anxiety, she tried hard to believe that at the Cradle of the Winds she could begin a new life.

As they sat there talking beside the fire, Siân learned that Frances and Emily Howard had lived in the shadow of the mountains for several years. They were never married, so had no children of their own.

"Do you live here all alone?" asked Siân when Miss Emily rose to turn up the gaslight.

"Through the winter months there's just Frances and me," the older sister replied. "And there's Father," she added, glancing up toward the ceiling, as though to suggest that he was resting somewhere in his room upstairs.

Listening first to one and then the other, Siân was told more about the rambling house where she had come to live and work.

For as long as anyone could remember, Crud-yr-Awel had stood among the hills and valleys of North Wales where the distant slopes of the Snowdonia range swept across the sky. Once a proud dwelling, it now showed signs of moldering with age. Its walls of tombstone gray were almost hidden under a shroud of ivy. And where, long ago, stately carriages had clattered to and fro, the stables had fallen to ruin and only a stony path remained. Shutters darkened most of the windows which once were aglow with light.

"Why, my dear," declared Miss Emily, "the stories we have heard! You could never imagine how once the house attracted guests from all over the country. Sadly those days have gone. Now there are only passing visitors who come to climb the mountains or fish in the rivers."

Too rambling a house for the middle-aged sisters to manage alone, they had recruited the aid of a young companion. Siân was to help with the household tasks, to run errands to the neighboring farms and village, and when summer came, to prepare rooms for the occasional guests.

"But most of all," Emily smiled, "to bring a ray of sunshine into the lives of three lonely souls, and a breath of fresh air to a dreary old house."

In return, Siân was to consider Crud-yr-Awel her home, and was to be generously rewarded at the end of each month.

For an hour or more they were together in the warmth of the fire while the grandfather clock ticked on. And the longer they talked the more was revealed of the old house's history.

Over the years many inhabitants had come and gone, each leaving the building more dilapidated than those before. Stories were told of rich landowners and their families, of intrigue and romance and tragedy—all tales likely embellished in their retelling.

Mr. Howard had brought his daughters there following his retirement. Once a sea captain, his voyages were now just memories, relived in the confines of his home. His spirit was fading like the ebbing tide.

Frances, who had remained silent for a long time, then rose to rekindle the fire. "There are tales of mystery too," said she. "There's many a heart would beat fast if only the house could whisper its secrets."

Supper was over and the clock had struck nine when Siân was shown to her room. Miss Emily carried a lamp and led the way along the hall and up the first flight of stairs. Shadows scurried about them as they crossed the landing.

Although Siân was curious to meet the sea captain and perhaps listen to tales of his adventures at sea, she would have to wait until daylight. He was now asleep, and they passed his door in silence.

At the far end of the landing another flight of stairs led to the attic. And there their visitor's bed had been prepared in a room with an angular ceiling which followed the contours of the roof. A low window, with a curtain trailing to the floor, looked out into the night.

"Now I must leave you to rest," said Emily, drawing

the curtains together and lighting the small lamp which lay on the bedside table. "Sleep well, my dear. You've had a tiring day."

She turned at the door to smile again. Then her footsteps were descending the stairs.

Not for the first time, Siân was left alone in strange surroundings. She put her belongings in the wall closet and changed into her nightclothes.

Even though she was tired, the thoughts that tumbled through her mind kept her from sleep. She kneeled on the floor and peered through the curtains at the hills and woodland silhouetted in the moonlight. Gazing toward the distant horizon and the sky above, she wondered how far she would have to journey to find happiness.

Crud-yr-Awel was wrapped in silence when she heard a voice whispering in the corner of her attic room.

"Somewhere from the darkness someone is watching!" the voice seemed to say.

And when she turned around she saw Faraway's eyes shining bright in the lamplight.

CHAPTER 2

The Talisman

Siân took the lamp from the bedside table, turned up the flame and held it high, until the light shone into each shadowy corner. It showed more clearly the faded pattern on the wallpaper, and a covered opening in the ceiling, barely wide enough for anyone to climb through. For a moment she wondered whether someone might be hiding there, crouched among the rafters.

While the lamplight flickered around, Faraway searched in the closet, peeped under the bed and behind the curtains. He whispered again. "Someone is watching, listening!"

The light was left burning low when Siân lay down to sleep, and it was a long time before her imaginary companion drifted from her thoughts.

On several occasions during the night she woke with a start, sitting up in bed to look around the room. Once she was almost sure she heard floorboards creaking as stealthy footfalls moved along the landing outside her room. She was afraid that at any moment the door would open and someone would come stealing in. Trembling, she imagined an intruder at her bedside, hands clutching her before she could escape, a pillow pressed to her face to stifle a scream. Then what should she do? Kick and claw, fighting for breath, until all her strength was gone and her struggles were in vain.

But there was no one—nothing to be seen except the glow of the lamp and the shadows it cast upon the walls. Through the hours of darkness no prowler came to her room.

The morning was gray. From her window Siân saw the trees in the garden and the hills beyond, all swathed in mist. Already there was movement downstairs. She heard the muffled voices of Frances and Emily, interrupted now and then by the deeper tones of someone she thought to be the old sea captain whom she had yet to meet.

Having no memory of her own father, she began to wonder whether he would be as forbidding as the foster father she had known and from whom she had run away.

Her fears were soon dispelled, for when she had dressed and gone downstairs it was he who called to her from the room where pictures hung about the walls, and where the grandfather clock still ticked away.

He rose from his chair beside the fire when she entered. And there, before a background of ships all embarked on voyages of adventure, she could well imagine him, bold and defiant, tossed in the angry sea.

He was a tall, lean gentleman, although his shoulders were now a little bent with age and he moved with the aid of a stick. His swarthy complexion was a token of his seafaring days, and there was a twinkle in his eyes as he invited her in.

"At last a ray of sunshine has come to drive away the

shadows of Crud-yr-Awel,'' he smiled. And then, with admiration, ''Why, no one mentioned that you had gold-spun hair and eyes as blue as the Mediterranean. Come, sit beside the fire and tell an old pirate what brings you to this dreary place.''

Siân sat on the edge of the armchair and felt the warmth of the blazing logs. ''It's so peaceful here, '' she said shyly, ''far from the noise of the city. I've come to help Miss Emily and Miss Frances.''

The old man nodded approvingly. ''It's a rambling old house, as you can see,'' he said, looking around. ''Bleak as a churchyard. And through the winter months there's never a soul darkens our doorstep. All so different from the old days.''

He was silent for a while, shaking his head sadly as though remembering happier times of long ago. Then he said, ''Perhaps we can persuade you to stay until the summer comes again. At this time of the year there's little here to interest a young girl.'' He lowered his voice, reminiscing again. ''Nothing but loneliness, memories— and ghosts of the past.''

''It would be beautiful when the hills stretch up to the blue skies, with no clouds to hide them, '' Siân imagined. And then, with tears misting her eyes, ''I've never really known a home of my own.''

As they sat talking together, the clatter of plates came from the kitchen where Frances and Emily were preparing the table for breakfast. It reminded Siân of the tasks she must begin. There were rooms to clean, clothes to launder, errands to run—all part of her duties at the country house. And with the hours of daylight so short she should make an early start. Hesitantly she rose from

the chair and asked to be excused. But she was soon to
discover that no one would hear of her working during
that first day at Crud-yr-Awel.

"Whoever heard of a new hand standing watch before
the ship is under way," joked the old captain. "Why,
you scarcely know the galley from the crow's nest."

He seemed in cheerful spirit for someone who was so
alone, and Siân dared to believe that her arrival had truly
brought a ray of happiness to the Cradle of the Winds.

"Someday soon," he went on, with a sparkle in his
eyes, "I will unlock my treasure chest and show you the
souvenirs of voyages to foreign lands across the seven
seas."

Siân smiled, looking across the breakfast table from
one to another, listening to each in turn.

"Besides, there's little to be done in the wintertime,"
Emily explained. "Nothing that can't wait until you are
settled in your new home. No one comes to visit
Crud-yr-Awel while the snow lies deep on the mountain
paths."

Miss Frances chuckled quietly to herself. "When the
days are bleak and the nights are long we are all alone,"
she muttered mysteriously. "But sometimes when darkness falls, when the moon is bright and the wind sighs
under the eaves, then, while we sit around the hearth or
lie awake in bed, uninvited guests come calling!"

For a moment the room felt cold and Siân was afraid.
In the silence that followed she remembered her fears
during the night in the attic room. Frances's foreboding,
the old man's reminiscing, Faraway's warning—all tumbled through her thoughts, and their words came echoing
back.

". . . memories—and ghosts of the past," the old man had recalled. "Somewhere . . . someone is watching!" her imaginary companion had whispered in the lamplight of her room. And who, she wondered, were the uninvited guests who came calling in the moonlight?

It was Miss Emily's voice that ended the silence. "Did you sleep well after your journey?" she asked.

Siân answered warily. "It's so quiet here at night. There are no streetlamps glowing in the dark, no voices or murmur of traffic . . ."

"Sometimes you can hear the bark of a fox," Frances interrupted, "or an owl hooting in the woods. As they watch from the boughs their eyes glow like lamps in the dark. And sometimes, when the house is still, there come sounds no one can understand."

Again Siân looked from one to the other, wondering if she should tell. "Last night . . ." she faltered. "Last night, when everyone was asleep, I thought I heard footsteps on the landing outside my room. I turned up the lamp and looked all about, but there was no one. I was afraid to open the door: afraid of what I might find waiting there."

Emily and her father were anxious to put their visitor's mind at rest. "Perhaps you were overtired," Emily smiled. "Wondering about your strange surroundings. Everyone's imagination runs wild in the quiet of night."

"It's the timbers creaking and groaning, just as they do when a ship is pitching and rolling at sea," the old sailor assured her.

But Frances's lips were sealed, her eyes downcast, as though she guarded a secret that no stranger should share.

For a while the incident was forgotten, and Siân said

no more of the mysterious sounds that had awakened her. When breakfast was over Captain Howard returned to the lounge—to the fireside chair and his reminiscing. For the rest of the morning Siân explored the rooms and corridors of Crud-yr-Awel, with the sisters Frances and Emily in close attendance.

Apart from the room where she slept, there were other odd-shaped areas on the third floor which served as a place where lumber was stored. Among the dust and cobwebs she noticed old pictures, faded in their broken frames, cardboard boxes packed with discarded clothing, an assortment of tattered books, children's playthings—all relics of past inhabitants and a time long gone: keepsakes that no one wanted but hadn't the heart to throw away.

A few rooms along the second-floor corridor were reserved for summer guests—the mountain climbers and nature lovers who came to explore the hills and wooded valleys. The door to each of these rooms was closed, and the sisters passed them by.

Emily led the way, chatting all the while. "We so look forward to the summertime: to the company of visitors—many from far-off places. Sometimes, after supper, we gather in the lounge and sit around the hearth. Father loves to listen to accounts of their journeys and recall his own adventures in foreign lands."

She looked out through the window at the end of the corridor: at the gray, November skies. "But then come the dreary months of autumn and winter," she sighed. "The long, dark nights and the loneliness."

Some rooms upstairs were bare, with shutters at the windows and only a carpet of dust to cover the floors. And there, when the doors were opened and they went inside, their voices echoed, as though someone hidden inside were calling back.

It was such a rambling house to keep warm and clean. Siân had visions of sweeping away the dust that had lain there over the years, of opening the shutters to let the daylight in, and lighting fires to take the chill from the air. She began to wonder why her bed had been prepared in the attic when rooms on the second floor were left unfurnished. Could it be that someone—something— along the corridor above the stairs might frighten her and keep her from sleep at night?

Into her thoughts crept the strange remarks of Miss Frances: ". . . Sometimes, when the house is still, there come sounds no one can understand." She remembered snatches of the old man's reminiscing: ". . . memories— and ghosts of the past . . . ghosts of the past." And there had been the warning Faraway had whispered: ". . . Someone is watching, listening!"

Near the foot of the stairs, almost hidden in the darkest recess, Siân noticed a door which she supposed led down to the cellar. She thought it had been left ajar, for she felt a cold draft which made her shiver for an instant. But on closer inspection she saw that the door was closed and fastened with a bolt. More mysterious was the sprig of withered leaves bound with red ribbon which hung from the lintel above it.

Frances hurried past without a glance, while Emily took Siân's arm as though she were anxious to lead her away. "It's just an old broom cupboard," she explained. "Frances is so superstitious. She has learned from old folktales that the leaves and blossom of garlic and a knot of red ribbon keeps away witches and evil spirits."

CHAPTER 3

A Chest of Memories

Throughout that first day at Crud-yr-Awel, Siân's eyes were drawn to the darkened doorway whenever she wandered along the first-floor corridor and each time she climbed or descended the stairs. It stood like a grim sentinel guarding some mystery that lurked beyond. When she passed that way alone she quickened her step, wondering what evil spirit might fear to venture past a cluster of shriveled herbs, bound with red ribbon and hanging above the door.

And as was usual at times of loneliness and anxiety, Faraway came to keep her company. Once, later in the afternoon, she looked down over the banister rail from the second-floor landing and saw him staring at the cellar door.

"It's always after nightfall when ghosts are said to come haunting." Faraway crept farther into the shadows, listening intently. "There's not a sound," Siân heard him whisper. He stretched his arm as high as it would reach, but his fingers could not touch the scented talisman that hung there.

She left him listening and wondering and made her way to the flight of stairs that led to the attic.

The door of Captain Howard's room was open, and he caught sight of her as she passed. "Ahoy there!" she heard the old seafarer call. And when she turned he was beckoning to her from the doorway, his face wreathed in smiles. "Come, search with me through my treasure chest. It's likely we'll find souvenirs of far-off lands across the seas."

A blazing fire warmed the room, which had high walls strewn with paintings of ships and scenes of foreign places similar to the pictures hanging in the lounge. His bed stood at the window which looked out over the hills. He drew another chair close to the hearth and returned to his seat at a table littered with various lengths and shapes of matchwood, twine, and pieces of material.

"It helps while away the long winter hours," he explained, proudly exhibiting the hulls and masts of a miniature craft he had designed. "Alas, my fingers are not now as nimble as they were, and my task becomes difficult."

Siân gasped with admiration, gently touching the rigging, the fine lines of the superstructure, and the delicate sail already assembled. Her eyes sparkled. "It's so beautiful!" she sighed. "Is this like the ship in which you once sailed the seas?"

The old man laughed. "It's an English three-master of the eighteenth century, from the days when my great-grandfather put to sea: when vessels were at the mercy of wind and weather, and every voyage was a dangerous venture."

Siân watched while he replaced his spectacles on the

end of his nose and with a steady hand fastened another sail to the mast, smiling with satisfaction when his task was done.

His chest of memories was of stout timber, bound with metal bands. It stood in the corner of the room. The hinges creaked when the lid was raised, and the old captain rummaged through the contents—an assortment of keepsakes gathered during his voyages of long ago.

Among his souvenirs were bundles of maps and charts, yellowed with age, ship's lanterns of tarnished copper, delicate garments of silk and lace, an old compass which had guided him through mist and storm, stones from the night markets of the East which had lost their luster . . . All relics of days long gone.

Siân grimaced as he took from the chest a fearsome curved knife and brandished it playfully.

"The kris was once a weapon of the Malays and Indonesians," the old seafarer explained. And then for a while he was silent, lost in memories.

"It was one of my first voyages," he recalled. "East-sou'east we sailed through the Straits of Malacca, and there we were told of an uninhabited island. Pulau Hantu it was called—the Ghost Island. The natives believed it was haunted by the specters of two ancient warriors who fought there over buried treasure."

Siân's eyes were open wide. "Was the treasure never found?"

The old voyager wandered back to his chair beside the fire. Legends were always embellished with their retelling, he reflected, but each was kindled by a spark of truth.

"It was dusk when we reached the shore of Pulau

Hantu and pulled our rowing boat up onto the sandy beach,'' he went on. "Although there was not a soul about, we kept a sharp weather eye as we crossed the cove and made our way along the hillside. And then, above the sound of the whispering breakers, we could swear we heard a crying and a clattering over the shoulder of the hill: a sound like the clash of swords, the shouts of anger and the screams of pain, as though enemies were locked in deadly combat.''

"The ghosts of the treasure seekers!" breathed Siân.

"Perhaps it was a distant clap of thunder and the cries of gulls, for when we reached the hilltop and looked around to all points, there was no one to be seen. There were only two stones standing black against the sky, to mark the place where bodies had been buried. And on the ground close by I found this crooked knife, its blade all rusted as though it had lain there for years.''

"And now the warriors' ghosts guard their secret," Siân surmised, "for only the brave would dare set foot on the shore.''

"Perhaps now the gravestones have crumbled and are overgrown,'' the captain replied. "But somewhere in my chest is a map which marks the place well. If I were a young man and bold as I was then, I would return one day to the island of Pulau Hantu and search all round a fathom deep.''

"Until you find the gold and jewels buried there," smiled Siân. "But now the gravestones have fallen to dust and blown away.''

The old man returned to the corner and put the kris back into the chest. After further rummaging he took out a leather-bound prayer book.

"There are some things hidden in the ground that neither wind nor weather can wear away," he told her as he searched through the pages. "Beside the graves grew rare tropical plants whose scent filled the air with fragrance. Because they bloom only at night and their petals are white and soft as moonbeams, it is known as the moonflower."

He opened the book and showed Siân some of the petals he had pressed among the pages. The color had faded so that they were as delicate as a web weaved by a spider, and too flimsy to touch for fear they would crumble away.

Carefully he closed the book and gave it to her. "Its Eastern name is the Keng Hua—the flower of good fortune. You can look at it each time you say your prayers at night."

He sighed and said, "I shall never journey that way again. I will leave the petals in your care, and the map I have drawn of the island. Perhaps you will be blessed with good fortune and someday find the treasure of Pulau Hantu."

Siân was overwhelmed, and tears misted her eyes. She knew that never would she travel to the far corner of the world to search for legendary riches. But that a kindly old gentleman should part with a souvenir so precious to him, and should share with her a memory he had treasured for many years, filled her heart with joy. She would cherish it for always and always.

The afternoon had worn on as she sat listening to tales of long ago. Beyond the window the sky had darkened and the orange glow of firelight grew bright. Before she left the room the captain lit the lamp and drew his chair close to the table, once more engrossed in his intricate task of constructing a likeness of the three-master in which his great-grandfather had ventured to sea.

That night, when supper was over, Siân went early to bed, for she planned to begin cleaning and brightening her new home the next day.

For a long time she lay awake, her thoughts dwelling on faraway lands. With stories of tropical islands and exotic flowers that bloomed only in moonlight still vivid in her memory, she had forgotten the mysterious sounds that came to Crud-yr-Awel after nightfall.

On the distant island of Pulau Hantu the ghosts of two warriors were said to return to the place where they lay buried, perhaps to relive their fearful struggle or resume their search for hidden treasure. As she recalled the old man's story, Siân began to wonder with some misgiving whether a lonely house standing in the shadow of the mountains had once been the scene of tragedy: whether here too a ghost came to search the rooms and corridors for something left behind long years ago.

And when at last she closed her eyes, Faraway was kneeling beside her bed, his head resting on the bedspread.

CHAPTER 4

The Uninvited

The day began clear and cold. From the window of her attic room Siân looked out over the garden and the hills beyond. The ground was veiled with frost, glistening silver in the morning sunlight, and the mountain peaks in the distance were hidden under mist. At the Cradle of the Winds there was not a breath to stir the trees, and the last of autumn leaves hung still. Siân dressed and went downstairs to the warmth of the kitchen.

"It's a fair omen that you should bring sunshine to Crud-yr-Awel." Emily smiled when Siân appeared. But Frances stoked the fire in silence. Their father was still in his room for, unlike the sisters, he did not rise at first light.

While the logs in the grate crackled and flamed, they set the table and prepared breakfast, with Siân helping as best she could. All the while Emily chattered constantly with questions and kindly remarks. It was so refreshing to welcome someone young and cheerful, she had repeated. . . . And they could scarcely remember when Father had such a sparkle in his eyes. . . . Had she slept soundly through the night? . . . They did so wish she would not feel lonely and long for younger company. . . . It was so peaceful there among the hills and streams, far from the noise of the city. . . . "And please remember," she went on, "you must go leisurely about your tasks, for there will be no visitors until the long evenings come again."

It was Miss Frances who touched Siân's hand to catch her attention. She spoke in little more than a whisper, and her question was followed by moments of silence. "Last night, when the lamps were out and the house was in darkness, was there nothing to disturb your sleep?"

With the morning sunlight streaming through the kitchen window, it was easy to forget any sounds that came in the night. "For a long time I lay awake thinking of Captain Howard's exciting adventures on a faraway island," Siân replied. "Then I fell asleep and did not open my eyes again until the daylight showed beneath the curtains."

She ate a hearty breakfast and then asked if she might awaken their father with a morning cup of tea. "It's past six bells," she laughed, imitating his seafaring jargon. "Time for his first watch on the bridge!"

"I'm sure that would be most welcome," Miss Emily smiled.

When she knocked on his door and entered the room, the captain stood at the window looking out over the hills as though he were scanning the foam-capped waves rolling before the bows. "Fair weather ahead," he announced, pointing to the blue sky. And while he recalled the winds and rain of the autumn now past, she laid kindling in the grate, set alight the dry twigs, and watched the fire glow. Then they sat at the hearth and

talked for a while, until it was time for the old man to go
to the kitchen for his breakfast and for Siân to begin her
task of cleaning away the dust that had for a long time
lain about the deserted rooms of Crud-yr-Awel.

"Just a little work each day," they had made her
promise, for they knew that there were parts of the house
that had been sadly neglected. "We asked you here more
as a companion than as a servant."

What happened next made Siân's heart beat faster. The
color drained from her cheeks and a spark of fear showed
in her eyes. Miss Emily had pointed along the corridor
toward the foot of the stairs. "The cloths and brooms are
kept behind that door in the recess," she had said.

"The doorway beneath the stairs?" Siân repeated
nervously.

Emily was bewildered. "Heavens, child, you're as
pale as a ghost!" She took her arm and insisted that she
should sit down to rest. "The work can wait until another
day."

Her sister's eyes darted from one to another. "There's
nothing to fear in the daylight," Frances muttered. "But
have a care when the sun goes down and darkness falls!"

Her warning made Siân more afraid. But she plucked
up her courage and, with some misgiving, made her way
along the corridor toward the foot of the stairs.

Quietly she unfastened the bolt, opened the door, and
peeped inside.

"You see, my dear, it's only a broom cupboard."
Emily had followed her, to show there was nothing to
fear.

When the door was opened wider and the light drifted
in, Siân was surprised to find no steps descending to the

basement. As she had been told, it appeared to be just a cupboard where brooms, pails and mops, and an assortment of cleaning utensils were stored against the walls and upon the shelves.

The corners were plunged in shadow, and from the confined space came a dank and musty smell as though the door were seldom opened. Siân raised her eyes to the cluster of leaves tied with ribbon. "I thought the door led to a cellar beneath the house," she frowned. "I was afraid that someone—something . . ."

Miss Emily smiled. "There's nothing to be afraid of. It's just an old closet. Frances has always believed in strange stories, and her imagination is as wild as yours!"

Many times throughout that day Siân passed by the cupboard near the bottom of the stairs. And as the hours wore on, her fears faded away. She had almost forgotten the charm which Frances had hung above the door.

Morning and afternoon she worked hard at her task, cleaning and polishing the rooms along the second floor—those reserved for summer guests and those left unoccupied. Most of the time she was alone upstairs while Frances and Emily were busy in the kitchen and Captain Howard sat reading in the lounge or had retired to his room where the model of the eighteenth-century sailing craft occupied much of his day.

Not until dusk had fallen did Siân gather together her brushes and cloths and decide to leave her task to another day. Nearly all the rooms were now clean and tidy. The floors had been scrubbed, the furniture polished, and when the dust and cobwebs had been wiped from the windowpanes, the red sky along the horizon was clearly visible. Sheets were draped over the beds and chairs in the guest rooms to keep them clean. And before she closed the doors she looked back into the rooms and imagined past visitors lingering there still, their white arms outstretched like wraiths.

As she approached the captain's room she could see the lamplight shining, and she called in for a while to admire his handiwork and put fresh logs on the fire.

Later, when she opened the door of the cupboard below the stairs, it was quite dark inside. She groped around to replace the brushes and cloths she had carried down. It was then that she heard Miss Emily coming along the corridor to call her to tea. Her footsteps came closer, but took a long time to reach the stairs.

"Miss Emily?" she called. "It's too dark to work any longer. Perhaps in the morning I can . . ." Her voice trailed away as she turned from the cupboard door to look along the corridor. There was no one coming toward the stairs. A light was burning in the lounge at the far end. But neither Frances nor Emily was anywhere to be seen.

Siân was suddenly afraid. She wanted to run from the darkness of the broom closet, but she was gripped by fear and unable to move. Somehow she was compelled to stay there, listening.

At first there was silence. Then there came again a sound like shuffling footsteps, followed by a scratching and a whispering that echoed from the dark corners of the cupboard. She imagined that a muffled voice was calling to her, but the words uttered were distant, barely audible, like the sigh of the wind under the eaves.

She stood there listening, trembling. And who knows how long she would have been held there in the clutches of a nightmare had not Faraway come to call her away.

He appeared at the foot of the stairs. "Quickly!" he urged, holding out his hand. "There's someone climbing the steps from the cellar—someone crying to get in!"

Frantically Siân slammed the cupboard door and fastened the bolt. Then together they ran along the corridor, and Faraway stayed with her until they reached the lounge where Frances and Emily were startled to see her come rushing in.

That evening, when the family sat down to their supper, Siân was unusually quiet. Her cheeks were pale and she glanced around nervously at the slightest sound. With her thoughts wandering from her present company, she paid little attention to the conversation around the table. Their voices seemed to drift into the background.

Miss Emily was concerned. "Perhaps you've caught a chill," she suggested, "working such long hours in those bleak rooms upstairs. We shall have to light fires throughout the house to drive away the cold and damp."

They praised her tireless efforts and wondered whatever they would have done without her help. But their tributes made little impression. Most of what they were saying escaped her, as though they were talking to someone else. Once or twice during the day they had looked into the guest rooms to see what she had done, to admire the clear windows and the freshly polished furniture. "It's a long time since the house has looked so clean and tidy," the sisters agreed.

Siân sighed, wondering whether the strange happening in the fading light of late afternoon was just a creation of her imagination: whether it was a mouse she had heard scuttering in the shadows. If she were to tell of her fears who would believe that she had heard shuffling footsteps in the dark—that someone had whispered to her in the cupboard below the stairs? Such things are told only in storybooks.

"Is there a cellar somewhere beneath the house?" she asked timidly, remembering Faraway's warning.

"A cellar?" mused Emily.

"When it was growing dark I thought I heard someone . . ." Siân faltered, not quite knowing how to make them understand. "It was a strange murmuring sound which seemed very near to me—and yet, some-how, far away."

The old sea captain sitting beside her laughed and ruffled her hair. "At Crud-yr-Awel there's nothing below the weather deck," he said. "I'm thinking your imagi-nation is as wild as a storm at sea!"

Frances looked at her across the table, her eyes glittering. "You see," she cautioned, "it's always after sunset. When bedtime comes I hurry up the stairs—and never without a lamp to light my way!"

Emily muttered reproachfully and her father laughed again. "Even when she was a child she was haunted by witches and hobgoblins," he taunted. "At Halloween and Walpurgis Night, the eve of the first of May, she hid red ribbon under her pillow and slept with the covers pulled over her head! Thunder flashes were a warning from the Great Horned God, and the howling wind was an evil spirit in torment!"

Siân did not smile at Miss Frances's confusion. After all, if Faraway—a ghostly companion from some Otherworld—should appear to her so vividly, who knows what other visions might steal into her imagination, and seem real to Frances too.

That night Siân's thoughts dwelt only momentarily on the mysterious happenings of the early evening. Perhaps it was because Miss Emily and her father had made light of her fears and showed how sometimes imagination can be confused with reality. Perhaps it was because she was tired after her day's toil. Whatever the reason, she was soon fast asleep, untroubled by dreams.

With the wooden shutters opened, the sunshine streamed into the room that had for a long time remained dark and abandoned, and Siân was proud to display the result of her labors.

"I can't remember when last the house was so bright and cheerful!" Miss Emily exclaimed once more. "The shutters kept out the light and made the rooms so dreary. We shall leave them open until the wind and snow of winter come again."

It was the farthest room along the corridor, with another unoccupied room next to it. At the other end, close to the top of the stairs, was where Captain Howard slept and spent much of his time studying his maps and charts and building the miniature sailing craft. Opposite was the sisters' bedroom and the rooms reserved for guests who came to visit in the summer.

While the sisters were examining the scrubbed floor and the shining windowpanes, Siân wondered whether they would approve of the suggestion that was foremost in her thoughts. "If I can find some curtains and a rug to cover the boards," she began, "then perhaps I could bring my bed down from the attic so that I . . ."

"Why, of course! And there's a fire grate to keep the room warm in winter whenever you wish to be alone," Miss Emily interrupted excitedly, wondering why it hadn't occurred to her before. She resolved to search at once for old rugs and oddments of furniture which would help make Siân's new room more comfortable.

Their search began in the attic, among the jumble stored there and forgotten. In corners and alcoves they rummaged, stepping around a disarray of boxes and packages. They came upon a creaking rocking chair which for years had stood still, a chest of drawers where Siân could put her clothes, a table with a rickety leg that could soon be mended, a rolled-up rug whose colors had faded, and in a box of discarded linen it was Miss Emily who found a length of old material which could be shaped into curtains. She took it downstairs and set to work with scissors, needle, and thread, leaving Siân alone to explore the memories left behind by past inhabitants of Crud-yr-Awel.

Many of the relics were playthings, once belonging to children who now had likely grown old. And as Siân searched among books and toys, old clothes no longer in fashion, and broken picture frames, she felt as though she were turning back the pages of time. Rag dolls lay limp, with tattered dresses and staring eyes. A rocking horse with tufted mane nodded its head as she brushed past to reach the highest shelf.

Resting above her head, among the dusty cobwebs, she found what she imagined to be the most precious memories of all. There was a hardcover book with its pages fastened together by a clasp, and lying beside it was a hinged jewelry box decorated on its top and sides with rough carvings. She raised the lid to peep inside, and saw an assortment of colored beads and trinkets. Underneath she discovered a little winder, and when it was fully wound she heard the dulcimer notes of a sad tune.

Siân listened until the lullaby faltered and stopped. Then she played it over and over, wondering what child had once been lulled to sleep by its haunting melody.

And while the soft music rang through the attic and drifted out to the landing above the stairs, she felt a hand close on hers. Could it be that once more her imagination raged like a storm at sea?

"Listen!" whispered Faraway. "I can hear a voice echoing far away. It's singing that same old song!"

CHAPTER 5

Memories of Long Ago

Siân was intrigued with the relics she had found in the attic. Again and again she wound the music box until she knew by heart the tune that it played, all the time wondering who might have treasured it long ago.

In the seclusion of her room she unfastened the clasp and looked through the book that had lain on the shelf beside it. She was a little surprised to discover that it was not a storybook with pictures and printing inside, but to find instead that it was filled with bare pages upon which someone had written their secret thoughts and accounts of incidents that had happened in the past. Much of what was recorded there had worn faint and was barely legible. Unlike other diaries, there were no dates to mark the years and months—just random chapters written in no chronological order. Inside the back cover was the photograph of a girl, and a name was printed boldly on the reverse side, which led Siân to believe that once the diary had belonged to someone called Sarah Jane.

The photograph was sepia in color, and the likeness showed the girl to be about the same age as Siân. She had large, sad eyes and dark hair which fell over her shoulders. Whoever Sarah Jane might be, and whenever she had lived at Crud-yr-Awel, she had not been a happy child, for there was no smile on her face.

Holding the book so that the light from the window fell on the first page, Siân was able to read what was written there, and from the start she felt that she had a certain affinity with the girl who had revealed her intimate thoughts. She murmured the words to herself, sometimes repeating those that were indistinct and guessing others that had almost faded away. Only then did the sentences fit together like the pieces of a jigsaw puzzle.

> It is such a . . . such a lonely house. Dark,
> dark. And the wind . . . the wind cries out.
> All the time it cries. When it is quiet the
> . . . the mist clings to the trees and the . . .
> the mountains are lost . . .

Siân remembered the evening when she arrived—remembered the house standing black against the sky. She understood then that it was Crud-yr-Awel the diary described. She held the page closer to the light and began another chapter.

> Mother's arms are . . . folding round you . . .
> Mother has gone . . . gone forever. Where can
> she be? He is a devil, DEVIL, DEVIL!

The last words were printed boldly, as though they were echoing from far away. Already Siân felt sorry for the girl—for someone she had never known. It was clear to her that long ago Sarah Jane had been alone and unhappy.

From downstairs came the chiming of the grandfather clock to remind Siân that time was slipping by and there was work to be finished. She closed the diary, leaving Sarah Jane to her fears, and wondering who the "devil" of long ago might be.

It was evening. While the sisters were busy with their sewing, Siân sat talking with Captain Howard, eager to show the treasures she had found. In the warmth and firelight of the lounge they all listened to the tinkling sound of the music box, sometimes humming softly, for it was an old tune they remembered.

"It takes me back to the days of my childhood," Miss Emily sighed. "Sweet memories of happy times, calling from years gone by."

But sadly, they reflected, it was only a plaything, put aside and forgotten. And the diary was a collection of hidden thoughts which, perhaps, were never meant to be shared.

"Ghostly voices from the past," echoed the old man, recalling one of his adventures at sea. "They have called many a seafarer to his doom."

He told Siân a fascinating story which the sisters had heard many times before. It was about the Sirens of the Aegean Sea, those mythical beings who, with enchanting voice and music, lured seamen to their rocky isles from where they were never to return. "They were never seen," he recalled, "but their calling was irresistible, sometimes little more than a whisper."

"Would a haunting melody call them back again?" Siân asked, remembering the voice Faraway had heard singing the song the jewelry box played, and wondering if the tune had lured someone back to her childhood memories.

Frances paused for a moment, her sewing needle poised, as though she too had heard a distant voice. "It's an old Welsh lullaby," she said, and then recited some of the words she remembered. "Breichiau mam sy'n dyn am danat—Mother's arms are folding round you." Most of the words she had forgotten, but she would always remember the tune.

As the evening wore on, many questions tumbled through Siân's thoughts. Already she had learned that the Howards had lived at Crud-yr-Awel for almost ten years, and that for a long time before they had moved to the county of Caernarvon, the house had been unoccupied. But the years beyond were shrouded in mystery. Sometime, somewhere, in its dark history, others had lived there in the shadow of the mountains. And there were times when Siân was afraid that their ghosts lingered on, haunting the rooms and stairways. Among them was an orphan with dark hair and sad eyes. And if her secret thoughts were true, she had lost her mother and feared some devil abroad.

That night, in the quiet of her room, Siân turned the pages of Sarah Jane's diary. She was reluctant to pry into her secrets, but, after all, they were written long ago— another time, a far generation. Perhaps now the girl was an old lady, or even dead and gone.

Not all of Sarah Jane's thoughts were of unhappy times. She wrote of the joy of Christmas, when tinsel on the tree glittered in the candlelight, when the robin fluttered to her windowsill and left footprints in the snow. She wrote of her rambling in the hills, among the heather and murmuring brooks, days of blue skies and sunshine. But there were grisly chapters too, which were fraught with despair. The writing looked even fainter in the lamplight as Siân spelled out the words.

It is cold . . . and dark down in the cellar.

Her heart leaped. Could it be that Faraway's fears were well founded when he imagined he heard someone climbing the cellar steps? Perhaps all the others at Crud-yr-Awel—Frances, Emily, even her friend the kindly old sea captain—perhaps they were hiding the truth, afraid to uncover some guarded secret.

> There is no one to hear . . . no one to hear
> me cry for help. . . . One day he will leave me
> there. . . . He will leave me there forever. . . .
> If only I could run away . . . far, far away.

At length Siân's eyes grew tired after peering at the faded writing. For a long time she looked at the photograph of Sarah Jane, studying it until the girl's features were vivid in her memory. The sad story of her plight began to emerge.

Once upon a time—no one could tell how long ago—there lived at Crud-yr-Awel a girl about Siân's age, whose mother had gone away, leaving her alone and afraid—afraid of someone who locked her away in the darkness of the cellar. Who he was, and why he treated her so cruelly, remained a mystery. But in her heart Siân believed that the girl's fears were not imagined.

Before she went to sleep that night she put away the music box and the diary she had found in the attic. They were laid to rest on a shelf in the closet of her room beside another keepsake she treasured—the petals of the moonflower pressed in the pages of a prayer book. And there they lay, undisturbed, while in the days that followed, Siân was hard at work brightening the rooms of her new home and winning the affection of those who sheltered her.

December began overcast and brought the first flurries of snow. Fires glowed daily in the rooms they occupied, filling the house with warmth and comfort. For the first time that she could remember, Siân felt secure within a home and a family she could call her own. No longer was she isolated in the attic, but had moved to the spacious room on the second floor, furnished with newly made curtains and rugs and an assortment of pictures and ornaments.

As the weeks passed by she tended to the household chores and brought to Crud-yr-Awel a happiness it had never known, and dared to believe that the Howards cared for her as they would for a child of their own. Perhaps it would be her home forever.

One afternoon, not long before Christmas, she went to the woodshed at the bottom of the garden to replenish the logs which were stored on a rack beside the hearth in the kitchen. She picked her way along the path, stooping beneath a tangle of briar rose branches and brambles which arched overhead. The lawn had grown lank and brown, sprawling beyond its boundary, and shallow drifts of snow lay where once there had been flower beds.

The door of the woodshed was open, and from the stretch of ground behind came the sound of someone

chopping wood. It was a tall boy she saw there wielding
an ax. He was dressed in coarse trousers and a shirt with
rolled-up sleeves. Unaware of Siân's presence, he swung
the ax with vigor, splitting through the bark and knots of
sawed-off boughs. A shock of auburn hair tumbled over
his forehead which glistened with sweat.

For a while Siân stood watching him, until he stopped
to rest and wipe his brow. "Who are you?" he asked,
looking her over. His eyes were hazel and twinkled
mischievously, his face freckled.

"I've come for some firewood," said Siân. And then,
noticing his puzzled frown, "I've come from the house,"
she went on, pointing over her shoulder. "From Crud-
yr-Awel. That's where I live—with Miss Emily and Miss
Frances."

"They've no relations that I've heard of." The boy
looked at her incredulously.

Siân felt uneasy. "I've come to help them," she
explained. "This is to be my home." She returned his
steady gaze. "And who are you?"

"David," he replied, rolling down his sleeves and
pulling on an old cardigan. "Sometimes I cut wood for
the Howards and keep the weeds from smothering the
flower beds."

He lived at Maesgwyn Farm over the hill, Siân was
told. Once in a while he came to Crud-yr-Awel to tend
the garden or to bring logs for the fires. These he gathered
from the woods nearby. Sometimes he brought trout from
the mountain streams or whortleberries from the hillside.
"Cutting wood is hard work for two ladies and an old
man," he said. "There's no one to help them—and
they've always been kind to me," he remembered. Then

he strode off toward the shed. "I'll help you with the firewood," he called back.

They made several journeys to and from the kitchen, with logs piled high in their arms. "You've not been here long," said David as they struggled along the path. "Don't you find it lonely here, buried away among the hills?"

"It's quiet," Siân admitted. "But it can be more lonely among the noise and people of the city when you have no friends."

"There's always brothers or sisters to keep you company—if you don't quarrel and fight," he added with a grin.

"I've no one." Siân did not mention Faraway, for she knew he would never understand. "Captain Howard is a good friend. I spend hours listening to accounts of his adventures at sea. He has traveled the world over—from snow-covered lands to places where the sky is always blue. But he says there's nowhere more beautiful than the hills of Wales."

When the wood was stacked they were alone in the kitchen. David looked up at the gnarled oak beams across the ceiling and the tall, open chimney where the sky showed through. "It's a strange old house," he remarked. "Hundreds of years old, my grandfather says. It has a fearful history, he's heard tell. No one ever stays long at Crud-yr-Awel."

A spark of interest shone in Siân's eyes. It was likely that the memory of David's grandfather stretched back for many years. "Does he remember who lived here long ago?" she asked.

David shrugged his shoulders. "For years before we

were born the house was deserted. That's when the timbers of the floors and roof began to fall to ruin, and the garden was overgrown with briars and brambles. A cloak of ivy crept over the walls and along the ground, strangling the shrubs and saplings.''

"Perhaps someday it will look grand and beautiful again," Siân smiled wistfully. "The trees will grow tall and the roses will bloom."

As they sat together before the kitchen fire, David told what he had learned of the house's history, but recollections were dim and broken. It was remembered among the villagers that after the time it had stood derelict, Crud-yr-Awel had been restored by Squire Mansel, a wealthy landowner in the county of Caernarvon. For many years he had lived there with his wife and servant, until his death at the turn of the century. That was when Captain Howard and his family moved into the house.

"Did they have children?" Siân interrupted, secretly wondering whether Sarah Jane had once been the daughter of a country gentleman.

But no light was shed on the mystery of Sarah Jane's identity, for David had heard no mention of a child in the squire's home.

He threw fresh logs on the fire. "Its fearful history began longer ago than that," he said. "I mean before the house was left to crumble away."

And so the grim past of Crud-yr-Awel—the secret fears of Sarah Jane—remained unknown. There had been only hearsay, David told her: only hazy stories of inhabitants who lived there awhile and then left suddenly, as though someone—something—had frightened them away. At that time many families had come and gone.

"No one knows for sure if the old tales are true," he said at length. "It happened so long ago. But even now, when the moon is bright and the owls cry from the woods, there are people from the village who cross to the other side of the road whenever they pass by the gates of Crud-yr-Awel, and many who say that the house is haunted!"

Siân looked about her. The sunshine came slanting through the window like the rays of a flashlight feeling in the shadows. The fire glowed in the hearth. Through the open door she could see the passage leading from the kitchen falling away in darkness. There was not a sound from the garden.

The time came for David to return to his work in the woodshed. "Perhaps the stories are just like legends—only make-believe," he said. "My grandfather says that ghosts live only in your imagination."

Siân went with him along the garden path. And as they walked together her thoughts did not dwell on the likeness of a girl with sad eyes, and an old lullaby played on a music box, but on a boy with a mischievous twinkle in his eyes and a shock of auburn hair that tumbled over his forehead.

CHAPTER 6

Christmas Eve

So accustomed had she become to her new surroundings that Siân could hardly believe she had been at Crud-yr-Awel for less than two months. It seemed only yesterday when she arrived at the gate and wound her way along the path to the shadowy porch. Since that time she had never wandered far beyond the boundary walls.

There were occasions when she imagined the house was a living, breathing soul, intent on keeping her captive. Was it truly a cradle of the winds, rocking to and fro, lulling one to sleep? For, strange to say, when sometimes she set off on an errand to the village, gusts would come whining over the shoulder of the hill, clutching at her clothes to hold her back. And on the return journey they would whistle and moan behind her, hastening her steps and opening wide the gates to welcome her home. More eerie still were the voices of Crud-yr-Awel that whispered to her after nightfall, especially, it seemed, whenever she passed by the cupboard below the stairs. There the ghostly murmurs were more distinct than in the darkest corners of the house.

Often Siân would stand at the window in her room, looking out across the hills behind which Maesgwyn Farm was hidden. Perhaps one day soon a boy with auburn hair would appear, plodding along from the woods, dragging a fallen bough. Then she would hurry down into the valley to meet him where the bridge crossed the stream, and would offer to help him with his burden. Day after day she watched from her window— but there was no sign of David.

"We shall barely have enough wood to last through the winter." Siân was piling logs high on the fires, not only because it was a cold December morning, but because when their store of fuel was exhausted more would be brought from the woods. "I wonder when David will call again."

Emily smiled. "The east wind is biting at this time of the year, and there are more fires lit now that you are here to help us."

"We should be thankful that the house is no longer cold and dreary as a churchyard," the old man said, watching the flames rise in the kitchen chimney.

And so, with winter upon them, each day passed with the house protected from its icy grip.

On Christmas Eve, Captain Howard was resting in his room, and from the kitchen came the smell of fresh baking and the sizzling of a goose roasting in the oven. As had been their custom in years past, the festive season was observed quietly. There was no longer the wonder and excitement that children bring. Siân had drawn the curtains and lit the lamp in the lounge when she heard someone knocking on the door. Her eyes were bright when she saw David standing at the threshold.

"I thought Christmas would be a special time this year," he said as she invited him in. "I've brought a present to celebrate your . . ." He hesitated, not quite knowing what to say. "I mean . . . Christmas is always so quiet at Crud-yr-Awel with only . . . Well, now you're here to keep them company." Awkwardly he took her hand and led her outside.

Along the path toward the gate they went, Siân confused and excited. "Where are you taking me?" she laughed, following in his footsteps.

"You'll see. Close your eyes!"

And when her eyes were opened she found herself standing at the roadside beside a cart, with a gray pony waiting patiently in the shafts. A lantern hung where the driver sat, and its orange glow fell on the fresh green needles of the tallest Christmas tree Siân had ever seen. Lying beside it were bunches of holly sprinkled with red berries.

She gasped, in wonder and surprise.

"Merry Christmas!" he smiled. "And that's my pony, Jess. But you can ride her whenever you wish."

Siân was thrilled as the tree was carried indoors and stood near the window of the lounge. Before long everyone gathered around to admire its outspread branches and the sprigs of holly hung about with berries as crimson as the fire glow. Frances and Emily searched their room for ribbons and baubles to decorate the fir tree; from the attic they brought a little doll in silvery gown which was fixed to the top as the crowning angel; colored strips of paper dangled to the floor. Then the lamp was dimmed and candles lit around, so that it all shimmered and glistened.

"The candleshine looks like harbor lights dancing in the water," the old man sighed. Frances and Emily could remember nothing so pretty since the days of their childhood. And for Siân, who had never known a family of her own nor a faithful friend, it was the happiest Christmas ever. Gifts were wrapped and laid under the tree, and from the old gentleman there were golden sovereigns, one each for David and Siân. Siân was moved to tears, for she had nothing to give.

"Remember, my dear," Emily sighed, holding her close, "there is no gift more precious than love and friendship."

As the evening wore on, David and Siân sat together at the fireside, watching the flickering light of the candles, while the sisters moved busily to and from the kitchen. Siân wondered why the spirit of Christmas did not last the whole year through—the kindness, the goodwill to others. For a while David and the old man were silent too, perhaps remembering how cold and cheerless the house had always been, each day passing as gloomy as the last, with shutters at the windows to keep the daylight out. Crud-yr-Awel then seemed as dark and sinister as when it had lain derelict.

David stoked the fire until it flared as bright as day, its heat burning their cheeks.

"Without your help there'd be only candlelight to keep us warm," said Siân. "Whatever would they have done with no one to gather wood and keep the garden from growing wild?"

"We're lucky the woods is so near," David replied. "It's you who's helped them most. Everything—everyone—has changed since you arrived."

He fell silent again for a time, memories drifting back. "I've never told anyone before . . ." he began. "Perhaps no one would understand. In the summer evenings when I worked in the garden, I always left before the daylight faded—like a gravedigger leaves the churchyard! I was afraid that I should see some ghostly face looking down at me from the attic window, or watching from the undergrowth." He laughed. "It's strange what tricks your imagination plays."

Siân was relieved to learn that it was not only she who had such a burning imagination. "Do you believe that the old tales—the stories told by the villagers—do you believe they are true?" she asked. "Do you believe Crud-yr-Awel is haunted?"

David lowered his voice to a whisper. "It is haunted by a ghost with blue eyes and golden hair," he teased. "She comes from a city far across the border to drive away the dark clouds and bring back the sunshine!"

Then they laughed together and forgot the grisly stories of some other time.

Not long after the grandfather clock chimed seven, the family were all gathered again in the lounge. The table was spread with savory dishes, oatcakes, and mince pies freshly baked in the oven. There were chestnuts roasted in the hearth, homemade ginger wine, and after several glasses of rum the old seafarer was in high spirits, recalling his first Christmas voyage through the storm-tossed waves of the Bay of Biscay.

"Tomorrow is a special day!" he announced, raising his glass to salute its approach. Then he took his daughter's hand and led her to a piano that had for a long time stood silent against the wall. "Come, Emily. Let us see if you remember the old tunes you used to play. It's been many a year since the house was filled with the strains of music.''

Emily held back, hesitating. ''Well . . . I do declare, the wires inside the old instrument will be rusty after standing idle all this time!''

She raised the lid and pressed a key here and there. Many were out of tune; some issued no sound at all. She sat on the stool and ran her fingers over the keyboard, until the faltering notes recalled old melodies. At first their voices hummed in accompaniment, then they sang the lyrics they remembered. There were sea shanties to take the old man back to the days of his youth, and well-loved carols appropriate to the occasion.

And as they sang, Siân's thoughts wandered far from the firelight and the company gathered around it.

While shepherds watched their flocks by night, she heard. And it was not the angel of the Lord she imagined, but David roaming the hills above Maesgwyn, with a crook to help him on his way. In the distance sheep were bleating, and a faithful collie was trotting at his side. In his care she knew that the flock would be safe from marauding wolves and deep snowdrifts. . . .

Away in a manger . . . The old man, in his reminiscing, had painted a picture of velvet skies in Eastern lands, with stars as bright as jewels. . . .

Her thoughts did not dwell on *Good King Wenceslas* in the splendor of his palace, but on an old peasant who braved the snow and cruel frost to gather fuel for his fire. . . .

In the warmth of the room they sang, sometimes sadly, sometimes merrily, following the broken melodies played on the piano. And when all the familiar carols were sung, Emily revived old hymns and ballads. Among them was one especially for Siân, for although it was written in a language she could not understand, she knew the tune by heart. The lullaby told of a mother's arms folding round her baby. Emily played it slowly, softly, as for an infant falling asleep in a cradle; and the notes seemed to drift from the room and echo through the house.

Although she believed it was surely her imagination, Siân fancied that, beyond the notes of the piano, she heard the tinkling sound of a music box. She thought that Frances was also aware of the haunting sound, for her eyes turned to the open door leading to the corridor. Could it be that someone else—someone from the mists of the past—had remembered the eve of Christmas?

The fire burned low, and the chiming of the grandfather clock marked the end of their celebrations. It was time for David to start on his journey home, and it was long past the sisters' bedtime, for they were always awake at first light.

The pony was still waiting patiently at the roadside, nibbling at the tufts of grass that peeped through the snow, with the wheels of the cart strewn across the shoulder. The lantern shed little light, but the moon lit up the road.

Siân stroked the pony's mane and spoke softly in its ear.

"She's taken to you," said David. "Usually she shies away from strangers. Come on, Jess." He took the reins and led her back to the road. "You can ride with me as far as the bridge, if you like. It's not far, and there's a bright moon to light your way home."

Excitedly, Siân hurried indoors for her woolen hat and scarf, calling from the hall to let Frances and Emily know that she was riding part of the way along the road with David. "I'll be back soon," she cried out. Then she closed the door and ran to the gate where he was waiting.

When she had climbed up beside him, David flicked the reins and Jess broke into a gentle trot. The wheels of the cart moved silently over a thin blanket of snow.

The hedgerows were flecked and glistened in the moonlight. There was no sound but the muffled rhythm of the pony's hooves and the creaking of the lantern as it swung beside them. The sky was clear, the night still, with hardly a breath of wind to brush against their cheeks.

"If there were no moon you might lose your way," said Siân, watching the road ahead merge with the white carpet laid upon the fields and hillside.

"Jess knows her way well enough. She's traveled this road a thousand times." David urged the pony to a canter, then handed the reins to Siân, laughing at the exhilaration that showed in her eyes. "Don't pull; let her run free. She loves to stretch her legs."

The ground rushed by in a whirl of snow, and Siân's scarf trailed behind her. Presently the road swung to the right and began its descent into the valley.

"Easy, girl," David called, leaning over to tighten the reins. The cart slowed down and drew to a halt just below the crown of the slope above the bridge.

David was reluctant to leave his companion on a deserted road so late at night, but Siân knew that should she feel afraid or lonely, Faraway would come to keep her company. The moon was full, and Crud-yr-Awel was barely half a mile away. Besides, she loved to walk with the crunch of snow beneath her feet.

Before they waved good-bye, Siân thanked him once more for a Christmas tree which, in her memory, she would always cherish; and, with her eyes, she wished that soon he would call again.

"If you like . . ." David began, and hesitated. "I mean . . . perhaps you would rather spend all day at home, but . . ." He pulled on the reins, for Jess was fidgeting in the shafts, and tearing at the ground with her forehooves, restless to continue the journey. "From the farm there is a grand view of the mountains, and we could ride the pony through the woods. . . ."

Siân listened eagerly.

"There are hundreds of sheep in the pasture. Perhaps in the afternoon, if the weather is fair? . . ."

"That would be wonderful! I've never been close to the mountains, nor walked through a woods." She could not hide her enthusiasm. "Would I see the sheepdogs gather in the flock? Is Maesgwyn far along the path beyond the bridge?"

David did not answer. He clicked his tongue to the pony and the cart started off down the slope. "We'll come for you," he called. "Soon after your grandfather clock strikes twelve, Jess and I will come."

Siân waited until they had crossed the bridge and passed out of sight. Then she turned and made her way home.

Happily, she trudged through the snow, once in a while glancing over her shoulder to see if the lantern light had appeared in the distance, climbing the hillside path. She remembered Christmas Eves past, but never one as joyful. They brought only memories of loneliness. Now, at last, she felt part of a family, and had found a true friend of her own.

Before long there came into view the silhouette of Crud-yr-Awel and the trees which peeped above its gables. It was then that dark clouds crept from over the mountains, hiding the moon, bringing a cold wind to sweep the snow into drifts at the roadside and to pull at her scarf. It was as though she were being drawn back to the house on the horizon.

CHAPTER 7

Maesgwyn

The gates of Crud-yr-Awel were open when Siân returned. Whether she had left them unfastened or whether
the wind had blown them apart to welcome her home, she
could not tell. But once more she began to wonder if the
house were possessed by someone—something—intent
on luring her back: to hold her within its walls.

The evergreens that lined the path swayed and whispered as she drew nearer the porch. Her thoughts were
filled with the events of the evening which had passed
and with anticipation of the day ahead, so Faraway was
not beside her. For some time now, she reflected, he had
seldom crept into her imagination, and when, at odd
moments, he had appeared, his lilting voice and misty
shape were somehow unreal: farther away and less
distinct, like a fading dream.

When she closed the door behind her, the house was
quiet. Everyone had gone to bed, leaving a lamp burning
in the lounge, with its light spilling out into the corridor.
There were only smoldering embers in the grate, and the
candles had been extinguished.

For a while she stood admiring the Christmas tree, remembering the shepherd boy from the other side of the valley, their ride together through the snow, and the lantern hanging from the cart growing dim as it wound its way over the shoulder of the hill. Then she relit a candle, put out the lamp, and approached the foot of the stairs. There the shadows of the banister rail moved across the cupboard door. Not a sound was heard, although the candle flared and flickered.

The sun shone on Christmas morning and the snow began to thaw. The hours passed slowly. Siân counted each time the grandfather clock chimed—eight, and then long afterward—nine, and then, following what seemed an interminable spell—ten. Would the afternoon never come?

Frances and Emily had gone to attend a service at the church in the village, leaving her to set the table and prepare the vegetables in readiness for an early lunch. And there was barely a moment when visions of David and Maesgwyn were not tumbling through her thoughts: the sheep roaming the pasture, the woods where foxes built their lairs, and where owls might stare from the tallest boughs, mountains swathed with snow. Captain Howard, whose legs were too weary to make the journey to the village, shared her excitement, painting a picture of the farm and the surrounding hills.

"The house is built of stone," he remembered, "and has stood for hundreds of years—older by far than Crud-yr-Awel."

Siân put the kettle and a heavy saucepan to simmer on an iron grill before the fire. "Does David have brothers and sisters?" she asked.

"They're a happy family, I believe, with several youngsters. And old Joseph Poulson—that would be David's grandfather—he has lived there since he was a boy, and folk say he was the finest shepherd in the county. He's too old now to tramp the hills. Like me, he sits at home with his memories."

Siân smiled. "There's nothing more precious than happy memories, for no one can ever take them away."

Then the chiming of the clock told her that another half hour had passed, and her thoughts returned to a house of stone which had weathered countless winters. She pondered for a moment. "Crud-yr-Awel" was "Cradle of the Winds" she had learned, and then wondered whether "Maesgwyn" had a meaning just as romantic.

"Maesgwyn?" the old man repeated thoughtfully, in answer to her question. "As far as I remember that would be known as 'White Fields,' perhaps because it catches the first snows of winter."

"Or perhaps because the hills are sprinkled with sheep, like daisies in a meadow," Siân suggested.

Whatever the reason, she could hardly wait to guide the pony along the hillside track on the other side of the bridge, and explore what lay beyond.

The morning wore on and afternoon came at last. The cart was left in the stable and Jess was tethered at the gate when David called. Before long they set off along the road, David holding the halter while Siân, with her feet in the stirrups, clung to the saddle, fearing she might tumble forward each time the pony lowered its head.

"Don't be afraid," David encouraged. "She won't shy or run away."

By the time they had crossed the bridge, where the track climbed steadily, she was confident enough to take the reins and ride unaided, looking around at the pale blue sky and the dry-stone walls stretching to the horizon through a patchwork of white and green.

It was a little while later, after ascending a steeper incline, when the farmhouse came in sight. It was bigger than Siân had imagined and stood as sturdily as a castle, commanding an unbroken view, with the mountains of Snowdonia towering to the north. She stopped to gaze around in wonder.

David whistled aloud as they approached the house, alerting two black-and-white collies who came bounding toward him, barking and wagging their tails. In close pursuit ran his younger brother and sisters, all eager to greet their visitor, for seldom did strangers set foot on Maesgwyn. Then they gathered around, chatting excitedly in their native language, with few words that Siân could understand. Curiously they glanced at the girl with flaxen hair who had come from over the hill.

There was Alun, a ten-year-old image of his elder brother; Mair, whose eyes were bright and searching; and little Annie, who held David's hand and shyly hid behind him. Each had auburn hair and a freckled face.

"And this is Shep and Nell," said David, patting the sheepdogs who now sat obediently at his side.

"Dere 'm laen [Come along], Jess," said Alun, taking the reins and leading the way home.

There were friendly greetings from David's mother and father, who insisted that he take his guest inside to the warmth of the fire. There, seated in an armchair before the fireplace, was Joseph Poulson, the grandfather of whom Captain Howard had spoken. He was a power-fully built man, with weather-beaten features and locks of silver hair. When their visitor appeared he rose from his chair and smiled amicably.

"Dadcu [Grandfather]," said David, "this is a friend who has come to live at Crud-yr-Awel, the big house across the valley."

Siân smiled in return, and told the old shepherd how she had heard of him before: how his reputation was known throughout the county.

"Crud-yr-Awel," Grandfather repeated reflectively. "That's a bleak old house for someone so young and pretty." He sat down again and leaned toward the fire to light his pipe. "I remember the last time I passed that way," he went on. "The shutters were hiding the windows and the house was in darkness. Quiet as a churchyard it was. . . ."

He said no more, for now the family had gathered around: mother and father, sisters and brother, all talking at once, with kindly words to make their visitor feel welcome. Siân was offered sweets and cakes, and shown the Christmas tree beneath which lay an assortment of paper and ribbon that had wrapped gifts from Santa Claus. She admired Annie's china doll, with lace bonnet and rosebud lips, Mair's new frock with bows and frills, and the stout toboggan Alun displayed, hewn from timber found in the woods and painted bright red. Of all the Christmastimes Siân remembered, she had never known such excitement and happiness.

It was still early in the afternoon when, with David to guide her, she set out to explore the hills and woodland surrounding Maesgwyn. David's parents and grandfather were resting indoors while, from a snow-covered slope, came cries of excitement as the children careered from top to bottom in their new "chariot of fire."

In turns they rode on the pony's back, with Shep and Nell running ahead. But where the ascent was steep they let Jess run free, sometimes holding on to the reins to help them to the top. To the north the mountains rose higher and higher, where clouds hovered over their peaks like sentinels from prehistoric times. Into the sky they towered, silent and gray. David told of a summer's day when he and his father had followed a winding path and climbed halfway to the summit.

"We stood almost two thousand feet above the ground," he said. "It was strange to look up into the sky, and from the same ridge look down upon the clouds."

They wandered on, turning to the south and east where the lower pastures lay, enclosed by a boundary of dry-stone walls. Shep and Nell pricked up their ears at the distant bleating of the sheep. The enclosure lay at the foot of a hill, sheltered from the north winds.

"In wintertime the snow lies deeper in the higher pasture," David explained. "Sometimes the grass is buried a foot deep and the sheep are caught in the drifts."

As they descended the slope and drew nearer, Siân could see them huddled in flocks like fluffy clouds that gather in the summer sky.

"There are hundreds!" she cried in amazement. "How can you tell when some wander off and get lost in the hills?"

"The dogs will find them and bring them back to the fold. They are born with an instinct and trained when they're very young."

Some sheep had strayed from the flock and were grazing at the far end of the pasture.

"Nell, Shep, dere [come]!" called David, proud to show their obedience and the result of patient training.

At his command they set off, loping down the hill in a wide arc, one to the left and the other to the right, moving out of sight for a time behind the boundary wall. Presently they appeared some distance behind the sheep, and in response to David's whistling they lay crouched low in the grass, awaiting his next command. He whistled again, and stealthily they came forward, the sheep now moving ahead of them.

"How do they know when to wait and which way to turn?" Siân spoke quietly, not wanting to break his concentration.

"There are four commands they understand," David explained. "They have learned when to come forward, when to move to the left or right, and when to remain still. Their instinct tells them how quickly or stealthily to move."

With his hand held to his mouth to help his voice to carry, he called first one name and then another, whistling the commands until the stray sheep had been driven at a steady pace to join the rest of the flock. "They are easily startled, and then run off in all directions," he said. "Sheep are timid animals and always herd together. Where one leads the others follow." Then he rewarded Shep and Nell with words of praise, affectionately ruffling their coats.

Beyond the lower pasture lay the woods, with the trees now stripped of foliage. There was no birdsong to disturb the silence, and the only sound was the crackle of twigs under their feet. David led the pony along while, from high in the saddle, Siân lowered her head from side to side to dodge the overhanging branches.

"In summertime," David recalled, "the sun breaks through the leaves in pools of light, like a flashlight shining in the dark."

As the woods grew more dense around them, they lost all sense of direction, and wandered on, picking their way from one clearing to the next. Shep and Nell were never far away, running around among the dead leaves and fallen boughs. The farther they ventured the darker it became, and when, at last, they emerged into the daylight, they had traveled almost the perimeter of Maesgwyn, from their view of the mountains in the north to the woodland in the west.

For a while longer they stayed together on the hillside, roaming among the gorse bushes and banks of withered ferns. Once Siân dared to urge the pony to a canter, while David ran beside her and the dogs barked excitedly. She was sad to see the sky darken and the day drawing to an end. "If only time stood still," she sighed, "then Christmas would last forever."

The lamplight was already glowing in the window as they approached the farmhouse; and when the dogs had been fed and the pony was settled in the stable, they all gathered around the table to a tea specially prepared by David's mother. For Siân it was a memorable occasion, for she had never known parents of her own, nor the company of brothers and sisters.

As the evening wore on, she watched the children at play, rocked little Annie's doll to sleep and helped her lay it comfortably on the sofa, tied Mair's hair in a bow to match her Christmas frock, and talked with the others of the beautiful views at White Fields—of silent woods, and of David, the shepherd, calling to his faithful friends. She recalled too the clamor of the city and told of her life there, although that sadness was now growing faint in her memory. How lonely and afraid she must have been, they imagined.

"But now you'll be alone no longer," said David, for there would always be the Howards to care for her, and a family at Maesgwyn for her to share.

Through all the conversation Grandfather sat quietly in his chair, his brow wrinkled in thought. Then, as though he had been searching his memory to recall events of the past, he said something which immediately aroused Siân's interest, for she realized that he was looking back on the history of Crud-yr-Awel.

"It was always a gloomy house," he reflected. "For years no one lived there at all. Come summer or winter, no lamplight shone in the window; no smoke rose from the chimney. Silent as the grave!"

"Then it was restored by a wealthy landowner . . . by Squire Mansel," Siân remembered. "He lived there for a while with his wife. That was before Captain Howard came to Caernarvon." She frowned, looking expectantly at the old man. "But no one can recall whether there were any children. And before the time it was left to fall to ruin, the history of Crud-yr-Awel is a mystery."

Grandfather sighed. "It was never a place for children. Folk say that no one stayed there long. Glad to move away, I shouldn't wonder!"

David's father and mother were smiling as they watched the young ones laugh and play around the

Christmas tree. If it were not for children, a home would have no warmth and happiness, they agreed. Without them it would be dreary.

A light was beginning to shine on the mystery, and Siân's heart beat faster as Grandfather Poulson continued his reminiscing.

"There was a child, I've heard tell. It was a long time ago, and forgotten now . . ." He paused, closing his eyes to roll back the years.

"Did she once live at Crud-yr-Awel?" Siân's voice was hardly louder than a whisper.

". . . A wretched child, they say, who was rarely seen. Then one day she went away and was never heard of again. It was all very strange!"

As she listened, Siân turned pale, and a name was echoing through her thoughts—"Sarah Jane . . . Sarah Jane!"

The old man gazed into the fireplace, still reflecting on the days when he was a young man. Then he sat back in his chair and stroked his brow thoughtfully. " 'Did the girl once live at Crud-yr-Awel?' you ask. I suppose that might be true, although at that time it was not a dwelling house. As far as I remember—and before the place was deserted for all those years—it was a tavern where farmers and shepherds quenched their thirst after a long day in the hills, and a boardinghouse, I seem to recall, where coach travelers to England and Ireland broke their journey for a night's rest."

CHAPTER 8

Sarah Jane

Though a hundred winters should come and go, Siân would never forget that Christmastime in the hills of North Wales, the first to have given her joy.

She was quiet as she and David walked along the path, leaving Maesgwyn behind them. In her thoughts she relived every moment, from David's arrival at Crud-yr-Awel on Christmas Eve to her waving good-bye to the children who gathered at the doorway of the farmhouse. Yet all her memories were overshadowed by recollections of a girl who had known many winters past, but none had brought her happiness.

"It's strange that someone should disappear and never be seen again," she said, recalling Grandfather's story. "Perhaps the girl . . . perhaps that someone was afraid. Why else should she run away?"

They were crossing the bridge and had stopped for a time to watch the moonlight rippling in the stream.

"If it happened all those years ago, no one will ever know," David replied, standing back from the wall upon which they were leaning and strolling on. "Anyway, it's only an old tale Grandfather heard in the village. No one can say that it's true."

Siân followed, pondering whether she should share the secret thoughts and fears she had found written in a diary.

"What if someone left behind a record? . . . She hesitated for a moment, not knowing how to explain. Then she began again. After all, she reasoned, David was her only friend outside the family, and perhaps together they could solve the mystery. "One day, when Miss Emily and I were in the attic searching among the jumble, we came upon playthings that had been left behind and forgotten. There were broken mechanical toys, an old rocking horse . . ."

"My father and I were going to build a rocking horse for little Annie," David interrupted. "There's lots of fallen timber in the woods, with curved boughs sturdy enough to fasten underneath. Then we thought a toboggan would be more fun, for all the children to play."

"I reached high onto a dusty shelf," Siân continued. "And there I found a little jewelry box which played a sad tune when the lid was opened."

David gasped in feigned astonishment. "Was it filled with precious stones and golden rings?"

"Only beads and broken trinkets. Beside it lay a book with the covers fastened together with a clasp. It was not a storybook. Someone had written on the pages inside, and the words have grown faint with age." She looked into David's eyes and lowered her voice. "There were no years and months marked on the pages like diaries usually have, but it told the secret thoughts of someone— perhaps someone who lived at Crud-yr-Awel a long time ago."

"If there were no names mentioned, and no dates written down, then it could have belonged to anyone."

"There was a name printed inside the front cover. 'Sarah Jane' it said, quite boldly. And hidden among the pages was a photograph of a girl. She looked no older than you and me, and she had long hair and big sad eyes."

"Then, now," David contended, "she could be an old lady, or even lie buried in the churchyard!"

They walked on, beyond the bridge, along the road that climbed from the valley. Siân was quiet again, remembering, wondering. On Christmas Eve, when the piano was playing, David had not heard the notes of a music box echoing the same soft lullaby. And how could she explain the voice that Faraway had heard singing in the attic? Were they sounds that were only fantasy? Did her imagination truly rage like a storm at sea?

"I wonder," she said at length, "if Sarah Jane is the girl that Grandfather remembered in his story: the wretched child who went away and was never seen again? No one remembers other children living there."

David's curiosity was aroused. "What secret thoughts are written in the book?"

"I've only glanced through the pages. Miss Emily believes it was never meant for other eyes. But it's clear that the girl was unhappy and frightened."

"Frightened?"

"She wrote of a dark and lonely house where the wind cries. That's why I feel sure she was describing Crudyr-Awel. After all, it is the Cradle of the Winds."

"On the hills in wintertime the wind forever moans and sighs," said David.

"It seems that Sarah Jane, whoever she might be, longs for a mother's arms, just like the words of the lullaby played on the music box; that's because her mother was no longer there to comfort her."

David looked at Siân closely, as though he understood how lonely an orphan sometimes feels. "Perhaps her mother had died and would never come back again."

Now that someone was sharing her interest in a forgotten chapter of Crud-yr-Awel's history, Siân continued her story eagerly, no longer afraid that no one would believe.

"Most mysterious of all was how she described some person who was always cruel to her: someone who locked her in the cellar. 'It is cold and dark,' she wrote. 'No one to hear me cry for help. He is a devil . . . DEVIL!' " Then she frowned and murmured to herself, "But that's what I don't understand. The house has no cellar, unless sometime in the past . . ."

"If Grandfather was a young man at the time," David argued, "then whatever happened was almost fifty years ago, and there is no one to remember."

In the distance the shape of Crud-yr-Awel showed against the sky. It was getting late and they hurried on their way.

It was sometime after Christmas when David called again. On this occasion the cart was laden with fallen boughs gathered from the woods. And that afternoon, when her work was finished, Siân helped him stack logs in the woodshed.

"Now there's enough fuel to keep the house warm through the frost and snows of winter." David was leaning on the handle of his ax and wiping his brow with the sleeve of his shirt. "You will be as cozy as mice in a bundle of hay."

"But there must be work to do in the garden," Siân ventured, fearing that otherwise her friend would not return until the spring.

"The garden sleeps through winter. There are no blossoms on the flowers; the bulbs lie buried in the hard ground. Even the evergreens wrap their foliage close around them until the milder weather comes."

"There are withered leaves to sweep away, and—" She was thinking hard, searching for other tasks that might keep them occupied while the garden slept. "And we could untangle the brambles from the rosebushes."

David smiled, put away his ax, and followed her into the house.

On the kitchen table Frances and Emily laid a pot of tea and a home-baked cake they had saved from Christmastime. It gave them pleasure to watch the youngsters eat so heartily.

Afterward, Captain Howard rewarded David for his labors and invited him upstairs to examine the miniature eighteenth-century sailing ship he was building. And while they were together Siân found the opportunity to fetch from her room the treasures she had found in the attic—the jewelry box that played an old lullaby and the little book that recorded the secret thoughts of Sarah Jane.

During the last hours of daylight she and David wandered in the garden, unraveling a mystery of long ago.

"See how faint the writing is; some of the words have

almost faded away." Now they were sitting together on a rustic seat, flicking through the pages of Sarah Jane's book, in turn reading aloud what was legible. Siân turned first to the chapters that were constantly tumbling through her thoughts: those which told of the girl's mother having gone away, of the longing for mother's arms to fold round her, of her dread of a cold, dark cellar, and, most mysterious of all, of the "devil" she feared.

"Perhaps she was kidnapped and held for ransom! Maybe some blackhearted murderer kept her captive, afraid she would tell of his deeds!" Once again Siân's imagination was raging, wild as a forest fire.

". . . a lonely house . . . dark . . . all the time the wind cries," David muttered as his finger passed over the page, picking out a word or phrase here and there. "That would surely be true of Crud-yr-Awel. But the dark cellar describes some other house."

"Could it be she was locked in a stable? There were stables behind the house," Siân remembered. "Perhaps they were cold and dark."

David thought that unlikely, for Jess's stable was strewn with straw, and she was always warm and comfortable. "Besides, there would be steps leading down to a cellar," he pointed out.

They turned the pages and browsed through each one, pausing whenever their interest was captured, and reading the words they could distinguish.

Summer is a happy time . . . skylarks sing in the blue skies . . . hills . . . soft and green . . .
From the bridge . . . sunshine . . . in the water . . .

"The bridge!" Siân exclaimed. "Then just as we
watched the moonlight rippling in the stream, so Sarah
Jane has stood there and seen the sunshine reflected in the
water!"

But David did not share her excitement, for throughout
the county there were countless streams with bridges built
across them.

> . . . apple blossom all gone now . . . orchard
> like a little forest . . . quiet here . . . all
> day long . . .

Siân knitted her brow, holding the book close to
decipher the writing and repeating the words to herself.
". . . a little forest . . . quiet here . . . all day long."

In her imagination she journeyed back in time, to the
days when Crud-yr-Awel was a grand house, surrounded
by spacious gardens. "Maybe in the orchard the trees
were dense, like the woods at Maesgwyn. It would have
been quiet there, and she could have hidden where no one
would find her all day long."

But from whom she would hide, and why anyone
should search for her, Siân could not say.

And so they remained on the rickety seat, pondering
over the plight of a girl they had never known and no one
could remember. Yet it seemed Sarah Jane and Siân were
quite alike really—lonely, imaginative, with the same
fear of having no one to care for them.

Until the light faded they stayed in the garden, picturing lawns bordered with beds of roses, sweet-scented
honeysuckle clinging to the walls, weeping willow droop-
ing low, and the golden chain of the laburnum hanging
overhead—all as it might have been long ago.

"Someday it will be beautiful again," David promised. "In the spring we will mow the grass and build up the flower beds with fresh earth and peat from the hillside. Then we can plant seeds and shrubs which will blossom to all colors of the rainbow."

He began to untangle dead brambles which weaved through a holly bush, while Siân wandered off to where once, she imagined, an orchard had grown. But now she saw only thick undergrowth and an oak tree whose branches spread over the boundary wall.

She looked around, but David had not followed her. She was alone in the far end of the garden she had never explored. It was dusk. There was not a breath of wind and nothing stirred. And yet, somehow . . . She was remembering that this strange foreboding had come upon her before—in the cupboard near the foot of the stairs, that first night she had lain awake in her attic room. Somehow she felt she was *not* alone: that someone was not far away, watching her!

Her eyes searched the undergrowth and the cloak of ivy that clung to the wall. Then her heart leaped when she saw a misty shape beside the oak tree. It was not Faraway standing there, but a girl in flimsy dress more becoming a summer's day, and she looked at Siân with big, sad eyes, her dark hair falling to her shoulders.

For several moments the girl stared. Her lips moved, but not a whisper was heard. Then she simply melted away in the gathering dusk.

CHAPTER 9

A Ghostly Tale

For some time Siân lingered near the oak tree at the far end of the garden while David was busy untangling the brambles from the holly bush. Though she listened and stared about her, the ghostly figure of Sarah Jane did not appear again. And when, at last, she went away, Siân's face was pale and she could feel her heart beating in her chest. Strange to say, she was not afraid. Where most girls would have been struck with fear and fled, she was instead overcome with awe and wonder.

In the falling dusk, David did not notice that the color had drained from her cheeks. He took the path that went around the side of the house to where the pony was tethered at the gate. Siân followed in silence. She wanted to confide in him, but she was sure he would never believe her story. Once he had told her that sometimes, when he was working in the quiet of the garden, he half expected a face to appear looking down from the attic window, or a wraith to come drifting along the path. But that was his way of describing the eerie stillness which hung around the house and grounds. He could not have imagined that a ghost would really appear there, but Siân's imagination was far more vivid. After all, the specter of Sarah Jane was no clearer than that of Faraway whom she could conjure almost at will.

"The flowers will come again," David promised, wondering why she was so quiet. "We will work until sundown when the evenings are longer, and when summer comes the garden will be a blaze of color."

He climbed into the seat at the front of the cart and lit the lantern, while Siân patted the pony's neck and spoke softly in her ear.

"When the days are longer," she echoed. Then she looked up, smiled her good-bye, and watched until the cart trundled almost out of sight.

After supper she spent the evening with the rest of the family by the fire in the lounge. Springtime seemed far away, when David would come again, but whenever she was melancholy the old sea captain usually brightened her spirits with his wise philosophy and tales of his voyages to distant lands.

"In two more months winter will be over." Siân had been counting the days. "February and March, and then the frost and snows will be gone. When spring comes, David and I will turn over the soil, plant fresh seeds, and bring the garden to life."

Emily laid her sewing to rest in her lap and looked over the top of her spectacles. "He's a fine boy, and works hard from morning till night. I'm so glad you have found someone your own age to keep you company."

Frances nodded her approval, and the captain said, "You should go more often to the White Fields over the valley. The mountain air will put roses in your cheeks."

They talked for a while of the rolling hills, of the children tobogganing down the snow-covered slopes, and of Joseph Poulson, the oldest shepherd in the county.

"He remembers Crud-yr-Awel before the time it was deserted," said Siân. "A dreary house, he says, where no one stayed for long."

"Frightened away by witchcraft, I shouldn't wonder!" Frances did not look up, and her lips barely moved as she kept muttering to herself. But Emily persevered with her sewing, and her father's attention turned again to the book he was reading. It seemed they had no wish to pursue the conversation further, although the history of Crud-yr-Awel was a mystery forever in Siân's thoughts.

"The old shepherd's memory goes back more than fifty years!" she said. "He has heard that this was once the home of a girl who was about the same age as I am. One day, so the story goes, she went away and no one knows what became of her."

Emily sighed as she struggled to thread a needle in the lamplight. "Perhaps she was a servant girl who wandered off to seek work somewhere else. You belong here, just as though you were our own daughter." At length she pulled through a length of thread and continued with her sewing. "This is your home. I know you will never leave us."

"Wouldn't it be strange if . . ." Siân hesitated, looking from one to another, but only in Frances's eyes did she find a spark of interest. "Supposing the music box and the little book I found on a shelf in the attic . . . Wouldn't it be odd if, all those years ago, they had belonged to the girl remembered in old Joseph Poulson's story?"

Frances was thoughtful for a moment. "Stranger things have been known to happen."

"Then she was not just a servant girl, for in her diary she tells of her mother leaving, and how she longed for her to come back again. But what became of them no one can say." She glanced furtively about the room. "Maybe, when all is quiet, a ghost comes to . . ."

". . . to haunt the scene of earthly tragedy!" said Frances, as though she were reading Siân's thoughts.

"That happens only in storybooks," Emily said resolutely.

Whenever the old sea captain laid aside his book and that faraway look came to his eyes, they knew he was about to recall some tale of his travels. And while Siân welcomed such occasions eagerly (for each story he related was lively and colorful), Frances and Emily would have heard it more than once before. It was then that they put away their sewing and went upstairs to bed.

"You will remember," the old man began, "that all sailors are superstitious, and although they would brave a howling wind and raging sea, they would tremble at the sound of the Cwn Annwn, Hounds of Hades, crying out in the dark."

"Something unreal which they could not understand," said Siân. "Most people are afraid of the unknown."

"Your talk of ghosts reminds me of a strange occurrence that has remained a mystery since the middle of the last century.

"It all began when an old Irish mail boat put in to port in the southwest of Wales. That was where the ghost which haunted the vessel first made its presence known."

Siân huddled closer to the fire, the light flickering in her eyes.

"Early one morning a dockyard worker went aboard and was startled to hear a voice on the afterdeck when everyone was below. A soft, chanting sound, he recalled, like waves washing on the shore or rippling against the side of the boat . . ."

"Like the Sirens of the Aegean Sea," Siân remembered. "Those who lured sailors to their death on the rocks."

"The captain of the vessel only smiled when the incident was reported to him. But stranger happenings were to follow, and according to the story these were recorded in the ship's log. In the summer of that year mysterious noises were heard coming from an unoccupied cabin. The bosun investigated, but nothing was found, and the cabin door was locked from the outside. Not long afterward several members of the crew reported that someone was heard knocking inside."

At this point in the story Siân's thoughts strayed to the cupboard near the foot of the stairs. Yet it was only she and Faraway who had shared that experience, although the door was always bolted, and a sprig of garlic hung withering from the lintel.

"The incidents were forgotten until . . . I think it was the winter of 1852," the old man recalled. "The log recorded that a seaman was charged with deserting his lookout duty. During the hearing it was alleged that the figure of a woman appeared on the afterdeck, beckoning to the seaman and pointing belowdecks."

Now Siân's thoughts turned to the quiet of the garden, and a misty shape beside the oak tree. "Perhaps sometimes," she imagined, "ghosts appear only to those who wish to see them—those who are not afraid. After all, they are only reflections of things that used to be: echoes returning from the past."

"Or pictures drawn by the imagination," Captain Howard supposed. "However, the skipper could not dismiss all that had happened as superstition, for even he admitted to being awakened one night by a hand placed on his forehead in the darkness of his cabin.

"Time and again both he and members of his crew heard whispering voices and a persistent tapping coming from within the locked cabin, and once a shrill scream in the dead of night!"

"Was the ghost ever seen again? It was strange that a woman should appear there!"

"That's true," the old man agreed. "It is only on passenger ships where women are found. Sailors and fishermen believe they bring misfortune."

He paused for a while to stir the logs in the grate, and then he continued with his story.

"Some years later the *Asp,* for that was the name of the vessel, put into dock for repairs. During the first night in harbor a sentry swore that the figure of a woman appeared on the deck and then descended the gangplank toward him. Trembling with fright, he dropped his musket and fled to the guardhouse. As he ran, the specter pursued him, and when it drew near he felt an icy draft as the figure seemed to pass right through him. Another sentry fired a shot as it drifted away along the quay in the direction of a cemetery wall that stood not far away."

Siân shivered involuntarily. She had not forgotten that

day—it now seemed so long ago—when she felt so cold
as she passed the bottom of the stairs.

"That was the last time the ghost was seen or heard,
for never again was its presence reported aboard the ship.
But the commander who was skipper of the *Asp* was
determined to search deeper into the mystery. He traced
the history of the ship and listened to accounts of her
voyages around the coast of Ireland. During his investi-
gations he made a remarkable discovery. He learned how
some time ago the body of a young woman was found in
an aft cabin."

Now the firelight fairly glinted in Siân's eyes.

"They say that no one ever knew who she was nor how
she had met her death."

"So, as Miss Frances says, her ghost came to haunt the
place where the mystery began!"

The old man laughed. "Unless some seafarers had laid
their hands on a bottle or two of rum, and the fiery spirit
had set alight their imaginations!"

As the logs smoldered in the grate, Siân sat there,
wondering and wondering. "Why did the woman's ghost
desert the ship and drift away toward the cemetery wall,
never to be seen again?"

"Perhaps there she would find lasting peace. Who will
ever know?"

It was clear to Siân that in all the stories she had heard,
the ghosts of those who found no rest lingered on through
the years, never growing older. The warriors of Pulau
Hantu returned to the hilltop where they had fought and
died; the woman whose days ended on an Irish mail boat
haunted the vessel for many years. Then why, she
wondered, was the ghost of Sarah Jane seen and heard

around the house and garden at Crud-yr-Awel? Now, more than ever, she believed that it was not her imagination. Sometime, maybe as long ago as fifty years or more, some sinister happening had left a memory, with Sarah Jane at its heart. And since that time the girl had lingered there. Her specter appeared in the garden; her presence was felt in the attic, and most fearfully in the darkness beyond the door which Siân had once believed led to a cold, dark cellar.

CHAPTER 10

The Little Room below the Stairs

The last of the winter months passed slowly. Heavy snowfalls came in February, and cold winds from the north left the hills glistening white and icicles hanging from the trees. Looking out from the window of her room, Siân could barely see where the sky touched the horizon.

With drifts lying deep upon the road and mountain paths, she knew that David could not venture far beyond Maesgwyn, for it was cruel weather for shepherds. During the day he and his father would have to trudge to the lower pasture with bundles of hay across their shoulders because the grass was buried under the snow and the sheep would be hungry.

At Crud-yr-Awel the days wore on. Siân rose early each morning to light the fires. Outside she had cleared a path to the woodshed to ensure a plentiful supply of logs, but the rest of the garden was held in the grip of winter. She could go no farther, although often she looked toward the undergrowth and the solitary oak tree where the image of Sarah Jane had appeared in the dusk.

Her days were spent about the house, keeping the rooms clean and tidy, helping in the kitchen, and, perhaps most important of all, being a cheerful companion to Frances and Emily and the old sea captain who had only memories to comfort him. It was she who listened to his tales and traveled with him on past voyages.

Usually the family retired early, and when the rest of the house was in darkness Siân would be alone in the lamplight of her room, longing for spring to come again. Often she would wonder about the secret thoughts of Sarah Jane. From cover to cover she read the girl's diary until she could almost remember each page by heart. Sometimes she would open the prayer book Captain Howard had given her and touch the delicate petals of the moonflower found inside, curious as to what good fortune it might bring her according to legends of the East. And occasionally the lid of the little jewelry box would be raised, allowing a haunting lullaby to escape. While it played she would listen, wide-eyed, half expecting to hear a voice singing in the corridor outside her door. Then, in her imagination, she would wander back through the years as though she were herself living in another century.

From the tales remembered by David's grandfather, from sounds and visions echoing from the past, and with accounts recorded by Sarah Jane herself, the story was unfolding. Images changed from time to time like pictures in a kaleidoscope, but now the pieces were falling into shape, although some were still shrouded in mystery.

It seemed that sometime, long before the turn of the century, there lived at Crud-yr-Awel a young girl named Sarah Jane. For a while she lived there happily, for she

told of summer being a pleasant time, with the hills soft
and green and skylarks overhead. Once she had stood on
a bridge—perhaps the bridge in the valley below
Maesgwyn—and there watched the sunshine sparkling in
the stream. She had rambled beside a brook and among
the heather. She told of a Christmas tree glittering with
tinsel and of a robin redbreast hopping around and
twittering in the garden as though it were asking to be her
friend.

Then came the time when dark clouds descended over
Crud-yr-Awel. In the pages of her diary Sarah Jane
described the house as dark and lonely, with the wind
forever moaning under the gables. Her story had no
beginning and no end, but was instead a confusion of
thoughts which showed her fears and sadness. Her
longing was for a mother who was no longer with her.
But what had happened to her was one of the chapters
Siân could not understand.

> Mother has gone . . . gone forever. Where
> can she be?

Perhaps the mother had deserted the girl, thought Siân.
If this were so then it was an experience with which she
could sympathize, for it had happened to her when she
was a little girl, although then she was too young to
understand. Maybe Sarah Jane's mother had been
stricken with a fever and died, and no one dared tell that
she would never be coming back.

Whatever happened, the girl was left in the care of
someone who treated her cruelly: someone from whom
she sometimes hid in the orchard and who locked her in
a cold, dark cellar where no one could hear her cries.

> One day he will leave me there . . . forever . . .
> If only I could run away . . . far, far away
> He is a devil . . . DEVIL.

". . . A wretched child," Sian remembered David's grandfather saying, "who was rarely seen. Then one day she went away and was never heard of again. It was all very strange!"

It was indeed a bewildering story, Siân mused. And in the years that followed, Sarah Jane sometimes returned to Crud-yr-Awel—as ghosts are said to do—to haunt the place where she had known such fear and sadness. For it was she whom Siân had seen beneath the boughs of the oak tree, and likely it was her presence that was heard in the attic and behind the door in that dark recess below the stairs: the whispering, the murmuring, the singing voice as the music box played.

It was strange that now she knew it was the ghost of Sarah Jane that wandered the house and garden, Siân was not at all afraid. Sometimes, when she was alone in her room, she even wished the girl would come to keep her company as Faraway used to do. It was the "devil" she feared: he who held Sarah Jane captive and turned her days to nightmares.

Apart from the pages of the diary which depicted the girl's imprisonment in a cellar, there were other revelations which could not be explained. Sarah Jane described a woman who always wore long black clothes with a poke bonnet covering her hair, and this was the fashion of fifty years ago.

> I will never tell Miss Jessica . . . never . . .
> never . . . If I tell the DEVIL will find out!

In all the pages of her little book no one, save for this woman dressed in black, had been given a name. Siân wondered whether Sarah Jane guarded a secret Miss Jessica should never share, or whether she was giving this woman a solemn promise. Should she interpret it as "I will never tell Miss Jessica" or "I will never tell, Miss Jessica"? But the secret she kept remained a mystery, for that was never mentioned.

More curious was a recurring reference to a door at the far end of the corridor which hid some mystery in the room beyond.

> Each night when I go to bed the door is locked
> . . . listen from the attic stairs . . . Someone
> is crying . . . Is it mother who cries? . . .
> The DEVIL locks the door to keep me out . . . Only
> Miss Jessica goes in . . .
>
> A light is shining underneath . . . but the last
> door is always closed . . . secret . . . hidden
> inside.

Here many of the words were faded and illegible, but a picture was emerging. From the stairs leading to the attic, Sarah Jane had listened to someone crying in the last room along the corridor. Beyond the door she was forbidden to enter something fearful was hidden from her. With a start Siân realized that if the diary truly described events that had happened at Crud-yr-Awel then it was in the room she now occupied where the mystery lay!

Most intriguing of all were the last words written in the book. Many a night Siân had lain awake pondering their meaning.

. . . and if I should ever go away forever, then
search for me under the full moon . . . that's
where I shall be waiting . . .

The words echoed repeatedly through her thoughts.
"Under the full moon . . . that's where I shall be
waiting." Did it mean that she would appear only when
the moon was bright? And yet it was only dusk, with gray
clouds covering the sky, when the figure of a girl with
long, dark hair and a summer dress came to the garden.

Through each dreary winter day and each lonely night
Siân never ceased to wonder what had happened at
Crud-yr-Awel long, long ago.

Further snow fell during the last weeks of winter, and it
lay deep on the hills and in the valleys. Seldom did Siân
venture beyond the threshold and never farther than the
woodshed. But whenever she made her way along the
path, her eyes turned to the far end of the garden.
Constantly she looked forward to the time when the snow
was gone and she could wander there again, to watch and
listen for the skylarks singing high above the oak tree. In
her heart she felt that Sarah Jane was a friend, as lonely
and melancholy as she had been before a shepherd boy
had come along from the White Fields across the valley.

"It's dark and musty inside!" Siân was standing in the
doorway of the little room below the stairs, with Frances
and Emily beside her. They had finished washing the
stone floor in the hallway and corridor and were returning
the broom and pails to their usual place. "Should we
leave the door open to let the fresh air get in?"

For a moment Frances looked startled. "As long as I

can remember it has been fastened with a bolt,'' she said
defiantly. "Otherwise it will creak and rattle and wake us
in the night. It's so drafty in the hallway, especially in
wintertime.'' Then she wrapped her arms tightly about
her and hurried to the kitchen fire.

Siân groped her way inside to replace the cleaning
utensils in the corner while Emily held the door open
wide to let a little daylight in. There was no sound in the
semidarkness. Not even a mouse stirred. Then, as usual,
the door was closed and the bolt outside slid across.

Siân raised her eyes to the withered leaves bound with
red ribbon which hung from the lintel. She was sure it
was neither witches nor goblins the talisman kept at bay.
Whether it be by the dusky light of late afternoon or
under the full moon, it was not they who came to haunt
the Cradle of the Winds. But now the shadows below the
stairs were as silent as a grave, and Siân wondered if the
presence of Frances and Emily had kept a visitor away.

"The wind has backed from the north,'' announced the
captain as he stood at the window in the lounge watching
flurries of snow blow from the evergreens. "Soon the
thaw will come. Then the streams will swell to overflow-
ing and the hills will be green again.''

Siân was becoming excited, for when the snow was
gone the shepherd's task would be easier; the paths would
be clear and before long, silhouetted against the blue sky,
she would see her friend from Maesgwyn come riding
along on his pony. What a joyous time they would have
working together in the garden when the spring sunshine
had warmed the earth and a host of fresh, green shoots
peeped through the ground.

It was one afternoon some days later when Siân and

Emily went again to the little room under the stairs to clear away the jumble of old cloths and odds and ends that had for so long lain cluttering the floor and shelves. Frances found work to occupy her time in the kitchen, for she had no wish to go rummaging in the darkness. Some places were best left undisturbed, she thought, and old memories should remain unstirred.

They carried a lamp to the cupboard because in its sheltered recess it was hidden from the daylight. Siân discovered that it was bigger inside than she had imagined, the lamplight showing the far corners which otherwise were unnoticed. From the ceiling and rows of shelves hung veils of cobwebs, gray with dust. One side was angled, following the contours of the stairway, and the wall opposite the door was stained with patches of damp and mold, its plaster crumbling away. The shelves and floor were littered with an assortment of buckets and mops, brooms and rugs. Wood lice scuttered about the boards and the air was dank and musty.

"It's been many a day since a ray of light shone in this gloomy place," sighed Emily. "Frances is loath even to pass by the door."

Together they set to work, sweeping away the dust and cobwebs, washing the floor, and throwing aside everything that was no longer useful. The chimes of the grandfather clock had rung out twice before their task was done. Their clothes were smeared with dirt, their hair awry. It was then that Emily stretched her aching back and went off to join her sister in the kitchen. "I'll hurry along to put the kettle on the fire," she said. "A hot cup of tea will clear the dust from our throats."

Siân was left alone to clear away the last of the litter.

She heard Emily's footsteps grow faint as she went farther along the corridor.

For a while all was silent. Then presently the door began to close slowly behind her with a prolonged groan as it moved on its hinges. It seemed as though someone were trying to shut her in, although she thought it likely that somewhere another door or a window had been opened, allowing a draft to come rushing in. The lamplight flared and then fluttered low. Was it her imagination or did she hear a sighing, like the sound of someone breathing or whispering close beside her? This was followed by distant footsteps and then an intermittent knocking accompanied by a faint rattle which, on reflection, sounded like a door latch being raised and lowered. It seemed to come from behind the wall where the plaster was falling away. But it was only her own shadow that moved there. She trembled as the room went icy cold.

"Is anyone there?" she whispered. And then, louder, "Sarah Jane . . . I know it's you. Tell me why you've come."

The haunting sounds did not return. Siân took the lamp from the shelf and held it at arm's length, searching every corner. But still it was only her shadow that moved about the walls. She shuffled backward toward the door which fell open behind her. The grandfather clock chimed once more, and the voices of Frances and Emily drifted from the kitchen.

It was now dark in the hallway and along the corridor, with only the lamp to light her way. She did not close the door of the little room, although she was sure that Frances would fasten the bolt before she climbed the stairs on her way to bed.

The glow of the lamp fell on a small boy peeping through the banister rails. His figure was now so faint that Siân could see right through him, but his eyes were still as bright as dewdrops.

"There is someone," said Faraway. "Whoever it is has come back from long years away!"

CHAPTER 11

In Search of an Epitaph

One morning Siân awoke to find shafts of sunlight showing around the edges of the curtains. The chiming of the clock downstairs told her that it was only seven o'clock, a sure sign that the days were lengthening and that spring had arrived. She opened the curtains and looked out at the clear blue sky. The white hills were now patched with green and the outline of the mountains was clear on the horizon. In the garden below there was a chirping and a flurry as birds darted from tree to tree carrying twigs and little tufts of grass with which to build their nests. Nature was awakening after its winter sleep and Siân could feel the excitement surging within her.

Her thoughts were so absorbed with the stirring of new life that the plight of Sarah Jane, the little room under the stairs, and all memories of long ago were, for a time, hidden away in the back of her mind like half-forgotten dreams.

After breakfast it was discovered that the pantry was bare, with scarcely enough provisions to bake fresh bread. So it was decided that, with snow lying only in drifts at the roadside, it was time to venture as far as the village. There was flour to buy, and yeast, and salt . . . "And new-laid eggs," Siân said eagerly, remembering the chicken coop she had seen beside the farmhouse at Maesgwyn. She hesitated for a moment and then added, "It's not far across the bridge and along the mountain path." She was quick to dispel Emily's fears that the path might still lie buried. "The sun is warm and climbing in the sky. The snow will soon be melted away."

So later that morning she put on her stout winter boots and set off on her journey. She would call first at the farm across the valley and go to the village on the way back. But, she hastened to assure them, they were not to worry if she should be late coming home, for David's family were so kind and hospitable and loath to see her leave.

Where the path lay in the shadow of the hills, snow-drifts were slow to thaw. But Siân was able to follow the track, picking her way around them. Before the sun was high the farmhouse came into view, with the woods to the west and the dry-stone walls meandering over the hillside.

David's mother was feeding the chickens when she arrived, and as their visitor approached, Mair and little Annie ran to meet her, bubbling with excitement. What fun it had been rushing down the slopes on their new toboggan; and wasn't the winter snowfall deep; and the poor sheep had been hungry with no grass to eat, and new lambs were soon to be born; and time and again they asked where she had been for so long. They chatted away together, with voices raised one above the other, the words tumbling from their lips.

The children took Siân's hand and led her indoors where old Joseph Poulson was sitting by the fire. "Sut

ydych chi, fy ngeneth? [How are you, my young lady?]
I am happy to see you again,'' he smiled.

Siân's eyes searched around but there was no one else
to be seen. Then Mother came in with a basket of
new-laid eggs. ''David is in the lower pasture with his
father and Alun,'' she said, as though she were reading
Siân's thoughts. ''All winter long he has talked of you
and wondered how you were getting along at Crud-yr-
Awel.''

David waved when he caught sight of her at the gate of
the pasture. It seemed that Shep and Nell remembered her
too, for they came bounding ahead of him, barking
excitedly and then jumping up to greet her.

''I thought the winter would go on forever,'' said
David. ''Day after day the wind came from the mountains
in the north.''

Siân breathed a deep sigh. ''It's over at last. Each
morning when I looked from the window I saw the snow
lying deep on the hills. I thought of you and wondered
whether the sheep would starve and perish in the cold.''

''They have their thick fleece to keep them warm and
they huddle together to shelter from the blizzards.'' For a
moment David looked sad. ''We lost two ewes, buried in
the drifts.''

From the pasture came the sound of bleating sheep
who scurried around in little flocks whenever the dogs
were near. The sky was blue, with clusters of high clouds
hovering over the mountains like pebbles on a seashore.
Once Siân fancied she heard the song of an early skylark.

''The winter is over at last,'' she said again. ''Soon the
wildflowers will bloom once more and the bulbs in the
garden will peep through the ground. You haven't

forgotten your promise?'' she added suddenly, touching David's arm. "This summer the garden will be a blaze of color, just as it used to be when Crud-yr-Awel was a grand house for squires and their ladies.''

David smiled. "I haven't forgotten. When the snow has all gone we will dig peat from the dells and plant new shrubs and seeds. Perhaps one day the orchard will grow again.''

It was afternoon when Siân and David left Maesgwyn. She had spent the morning among the sheep and shepherds, and David's father insisted that she share a midday meal with the family, and that afterward David should accompany her on her errand to the village. "The track down the hillside to the bridge can be treacherous after a severe winter,'' he told her.

The warmth of a happy family gathered together was an experience Siân would always treasure, for she had never known brothers and sisters of her own. The children chattered incessantly, each with a story to tell. What fun it had been fighting with snowballs and building a snowman who, sadly, had now melted away; and they would never forget Nell and Shep foraging beneath deep drifts, emerging with scraggy tails and white noses. In turn they relived winter memories of blazing fires and the north wind howling in the chimney, of swirling flakes and icicles clutching at the window-panes.

Before she and David set off down the hillside, Siân went into the stable with an affectionate word and a handful of sugar for Jess. And there was a promise for little Annie, who begged that she should stay. "One day soon, when the snow has all gone away, your David will bring his pony and cart to the Cradle of the Winds across the valley. And when he returns there will be a special surprise for you.''

The little girl's eyes were opened wide.

"Resting in our attic, with no one to be his friend, is a rocking horse as tall as you. There it has stood, sad and lonely, for a long, long time—perhaps as long ago as when your grandfather was a boy. I don't know his name, but I know he's waiting for someone to climb into the saddle and go galloping over the mountains.''

The church and the cemetery beyond marked the edge of the village. They had left the shops, a sprinkling of houses, and the rows of terraced cottages behind them and made their way along the road to Crud-yr-Awel, laden with provisions for the pantry and an assortment of seeds which would soon bring color to the garden. There were still many hours before the sun went down and the fluffy clouds on the horizon turned red.

"I wonder if Sarah Jane lies buried there," said Siân absently as they stopped to look through the railings which surrounded the churchyard.

"Sarah Jane?" David frowned.

"In her little book she has shown us glimpses of her fears and sadness, but no one knows what became of her.''

David walked silently beside her, wondering what spark had set her imagination on fire. He followed as she opened the gate and wandered for a while among the tombstones, searching for an epitaph which might say: "Here lies the body of Sarah Jane ———, born 18– and died 18– Rest in Peace.''

Many of the stones standing upon the graves had moldered with age, their epitaphs faint and covered with moss. Some mounds were marked with a simple wooden cross while others were bare, perhaps because there was no one to remember.

"Search for me under the full moon," Siân murmured to herself, "that's where I shall be waiting."

Once more David wore a puzzled frown.

"It's written in Sarah Jane's diary," she explained. "Through the winter I've read her little book from cover to cover."

She strayed farther from the path, away from the shelter of the yew trees, for there the full light of the moon did not shine upon the graves.

"So many years have passed since then that Sarah Jane would now be an old lady," David argued. "Perhaps she is still alive and living far away from North Wales."

Steadfastly Siân's search continued. From stone to stone she passed, stooping low to examine the inscription carved above each resting place: from those who had lived far beyond their threescore years and ten to others stricken barely a season after their lives had begun. But she found no epitaph in memory of Sarah Jane. If she were dead and buried, then her body lay in an unmarked grave.

Patiently David strolled along beside her. "Someday," he foretold with feigned solemnity, "when we're old and gray, we might lie here under the afternoon sun. Perhaps we shall be laid to rest side by side—an old shepherd of Maesgwyn and a dreamer from Crud-yr-Awel!"

When their wandering was over, they left the church-yard and hurried along the road.

Frances and Emily were relieved to see Siân safely home again, and thankful to David for accompanying her. "You were away a long time," Emily said anxiously. "We were afraid you might have been stranded on the hillside. The drifts can be so deep in the sheltered dells."

"While there are stars or the sun in the sky voyagers are never lost," declared the old seafarer. "Besides, she had a good navigator to keep her on course," he added, winking at David.

Frances took the bag of provisions and stoked up the fire, for there was much baking to be done before the day was over.

The afternoon wore on. While Frances and Emily were busy in the kitchen, David and Siân spent their time idly. For a while they listened to Captain Howard's memorable account of blizzards during the winter of 1887 when the Irish Sea raged and many vessels foundered with all hands. And when his reminiscing was over they sauntered around the garden, planning where the flower beds should lay and where the rambler roses should cling to trellised archways. There would be a rock garden in the corner of the lawn, filled with white and purple heather and clumps of primroses. And lying below would be a little lily pond with petals spread upon the water as delicate as the moonflower from Eastern lands. Around the walls where now the ivy clung would hang garlands of honeysuckle and wisteria.

"It shall be our garden," said Siân, already imagining leisurely summer evenings when they would wander along the paths, admiring the verdant lawn and the blaze of color all around.

"Each day I will come," David promised, "when my work is done and the weather is fair. Sometimes perhaps Alun and Mair will come along to help. We always think of the mountains and the rolling hills as our garden. Father has a vegetable plot, but we have never had a flower garden of our own. Our flowers are the broom and the gorse and the wild mountain heather."

The far end of the garden, beneath the wall and the boughs of the oak tree, was still patched with snow. Often during their sauntering Siân's eyes strayed there. The sun had not yet fallen below the horizon, so dusk had not descended and it would be many hours before they saw the moonlight. She wondered whether next summer, when the garden was in full bloom, a girl from long ago would share the fragrance of the roses and honeysuckle.

She had no way of knowing then that long before the summer came Sarah Jane would return to haunt her: not at the far end of the garden where once an orchard grew, but within the walls of Crud-yr-Awel. And her presence there would herald a chain of events so fearful and mysterious that even in her wildest thoughts Siân could not have imagined.

CHAPTER 12

"The House Will Be Filled with Demons"

It all began a few days later when David came with his pony and cart. He brought with him sacks of peat which he had dug from a hollow in the hills, and large stones for the rockery found in the stream near the bridge.

While the daylight lasted he and Siân worked in the garden, digging the peat into the flower beds and building a mound of earth in the corner of the lawn. Using a rickety old wheelbarrow which had long lain idle in the woodshed, they moved the heavy stones from the cart and set them upon the rockery until it looked as natural as a craggy hillock. The flower beds surrounding the lawn were tilled and raked in readiness for sowing new seeds.

When dusk fell and their evening's work was finished, they stayed for a while to admire the fruits of their labor.

"How long will it be before the seeds peep above the ground?" Siân asked eagerly.

David was amused to see the excitement in her eyes. "With the rain showers and sunshine of April they will soon appear."

"Will there be poppies and forget-me-nots like the red

"The House Will Be Filled with Demons" 99

and blue of sunset, and daffodils and crocuses all colors of the rainbow?''

"And snowdrops as shy and pretty as you," David smiled again.

The snow had all melted away and already fresh blades of grass were showing in the lawn.

"Later on we will dig out the undergrowth from the far end," he said, "and lay new turf from the hillside. Then the garden will look bigger and there'll be no weeds to strangle the flowers and take the goodness from the soil."

They were hungry and thirsty after their evening's work and enjoyed an early supper Frances and Emily had prepared for them in the kitchen.

Before David set off on his journey home Siân led him to the attic, and together they carried down the rocking horse she had promised to little Annie.

"Goodness knows how long it has lain there among the jumble," Emily had said. "It gave someone pleasure once upon a time, but now it only gathers dust. You're quite welcome to any playthings that would amuse your little ones, although they're all old and broken."

So saying she had gone about her business, leaving Siân and David to explore at their leisure the relics stored in the attic.

It was when they had reached the bottom of the stairs that David caught sight of the door in the darkened recess. "A charm to keep the witches away," he recalled, noticing the withered leaves bound with red ribbon which hung from the lintel. "On Halloween my old granny used to fasten a knot of red ribbon to the baby's crib, and a bunch of garlic above the threshold. 'To keep away the evil spirits,' she always used to say.''

He laid down the rocking horse and went deeper into the shadows.

''When I am alone I hear strange sounds coming from inside.'' Siân lowered her voice, wondering still at the mystery of it all. ''It's just a broom cupboard, Emily says—a little room where cleaning things are kept. But when I am there by myself I feel that someone is beside me. Someone . . .'' She shrugged, knowing he would never understand.

David slid the bolt, opened the door wide, and peered from the entrance. Siân was looking over his shoulder. It was dark inside—too dark even to see the outline of the wall and shelving.

''Is there a lamp?'' asked David, going farther into the darkness.

There was a candle and some matches on the top shelf, Siân remembered. She groped around until she found them, and when the candle flame grew tall they looked into each corner. Everything was just as it had been left, although she half expected to find brooms and pails strewn about the floor as if some poltergeist had been at mischief there.

''There's no window and the door is always closed,'' David frowned. ''No wonder it's so damp and moldy with no fresh air and daylight getting in. See how the wall is crumbling.'' He pointed to the wall directly opposite the door where the plaster bubbled and was stained green with mold. At his touch large patches fell away, exposing the bare bricks behind. These too were wet and had worn loose, with tentacles of mildew, gray as cobwebs, creeping upward from the floor.

"Why, it's rotting away!" said David, loosening first one brick and then another.

It was then that they made a discovery which caused Siân to gasp with surprise. They looked at each other, wide-eyed in the candlelight, for behind the brickwork they found a wooden obstruction attached to which was a rusty latch.

"It's an old door!" David exclaimed.

"A door leading to a cellar!" whispered Siân.

It was too late then to explore what lay beyond, but they looked forward to the next day with awe and excitement. With some misgiving they wondered what mystery lurked below the cellar steps.

Siân stood at the gate watching as the cart bearing an old rocking horse, a china doll, and a few broken mechanical toys for little Annie trundled along the road. She watched until the lantern grew faint in the distance.

They had decided that, for a while, they would tell no one what they had found. Siân knew that if Miss Frances were to learn that something other than a musty little room for brooms and pails lay beyond her witch's charm, she would lie awake in torment all through the night.

Siân tossed and turned uneasily in her bed. There was no wind to rustle the trees and sigh under the gables. The grandfather clock told her when each half hour had passed. The moon was full, and she had left her curtains open so that the light should shine into her room. Unable to sleep, she began murmuring to herself. "Under the full moon, that's where I shall be waiting," she recalled over and over again. And now the moon was like a silver coin in the sky! She imagined that sometime before the dawn her door would open and the figure of a girl with hair falling to her shoulders would come stealing in. The intruder would sit at the foot of her bed and tell a sad tale of long ago. Perhaps the lid of a little jewelry box would be opened and they would listen together to the lullaby it played.

But no one came to visit her in the moonlight. At last she fell into a fitful sleep.

She could not tell whether she had awakened from a dream or whether the fearful cry that echoed through the house was real. It was the plaintive call of someone in torment and came from somewhere downstairs. The cry was loud enough to rouse the household, yet when she peeped along the corridor she saw that the doors remained closed. For a minute or two she listened there, but it did not come again.

It seemed as though the next day would never dawn. Before she returned to her bed she spent a long time looking out from her window, watching the full moon which shone over the countryside for miles around. If it were under its light where Sarah Jane was waiting, then she could be in the hills or valleys or woods—anywhere from the mountains to the sea.

Although the weather was fair, David and Siân did not work in the garden the following evening, for there was a more intriguing mission to explore. They took a lamp to the little room under the stairs and set about their task furtively. They knew that before long the others would learn of their discovery, but Siân wanted to keep their secret until the mystery that lay beneath Crud-yr-Awel had been uncovered.

"David is tending to the wall which is crumbling away," she called from behind the closed door when Frances and Emily wondered what they were about. "And the room is clouded with dust!"

So moldered were the plaster and bricks which hid the entrance to the cellar that they were easily dislodged, revealing a stouter wall of stone in which the door was set. When the door itself was fully exposed, their excitement grew as though they were about to enter an Aladdin's Cave. Its latch and bolt were covered with rust and seized fast, and it was with difficulty that they wrenched it free. They hesitated for a while, not daring to push the door open: wondering what they would find beyond. Their eyes met through the dust and lamp shine.

"How many years have gone by since someone last passed through this doorway!" said Siân, imagining a frightened girl imprisoned there in the darkness, crying out to be set free. It was here, she reflected with a shudder, that the "DEVIL" had stood, bolting the door to keep his captive in and stifle the cries for help.

At length the door opened with a creak and a black pit appeared at their feet. A cold draft rose from its depths, causing the lamplight to flicker. A flight of stone steps with a handrail at its edge led down into the cellar. David went ahead, holding the lamp at arm's length. Siân followed, peering into the shadows, her heart beating fast.

"It's as dark and quiet as a tomb!" David whispered, watching hidden alcoves creeping into view.

In one corner water had seeped in and lay in a pool over the sunken flagstones. In another were several small barrels whose hoops had broken away and the staves were sprawled upon the floor like monstrous spiders crawling there.

At the foot of the steps David shone the lamp all round. "Perhaps long ago the cellar was used as a smugglers' cave," he said. "Tobacco and barrels of brandy for the squires, and a chest of lace and linen for their ladies."

But they knew that Crud-yr-Awel was far from the coves to the north of Cardigan Bay and an unlikely place for a smugglers' hoard.

"It was a forgotten place, like a dungeon, where Sarah Jane was locked away!" Siân was sure. "It was here where the DEVIL—whoever he was—kept her hidden out of sight!" Yet nowhere in her diary had the girl explained why her tormentor should treat her so cruelly.

Now that the cellar had been discovered, it was clear that Crud-yr-Awel was the scene of the grim happenings of the past. But there were still other mysteries unsolved—Miss Jessica in her long black clothes and poke bonnet, the room at the end of the corridor upstairs with its door always closed and where Sarah Jane was forbidden to enter. And, most mysterious of all, the place under the full moon where she would be waiting.

Later that afternoon their discovery was made known to the others. While David stood halfway down the cellar steps shining the lamp into the darkness, they gathered together to stare and wonder.

"I do declare!" breathed Emily with a sudden shiver. "A dark and silent vault lying beneath us all this time! Whoever would have thought! . . ."

The captain wondered what sinister deed had been hidden over the years behind the concealed entrance.

"We shall batten down the hatch again!" he declared. "Then none of the past shall escape."

Even in the dim light of the lamp it could be seen that the color had drained from Frances's cheeks. She wrapped her shawl about her shoulders and shrank back from the cellar steps.

"The house will be filled with demons!" she cried, as though some Pandora's box had been opened and evil spirits had broken free.

CHAPTER 13

Ghosts from Long Ago

There were no witches or demons lurking in the cellar beneath Crud-yr-Awel. It was not evil spirits that would escape now that its hidden entrance had been discovered and a light had broken the darkness of half a century or more. In her heart Siân knew this to be true. It was the ghost of an unhappy girl that haunted the house and garden. It was her voice she had heard echoing through the corridors when all was quiet and she was alone.

On the table beside her bed rested the photograph of Sarah Jane and the little book in which she had written her secret thoughts. Each night before she went to sleep she had searched through the pages recalling the fears and sadness of a girl who had lived there long ago. Often she had gazed at her picture until she remembered the expression in her eyes, every line in her face. Sometimes, when she held it close and wrinkled her eyes, it seemed that Sarah Jane was there before her, staring back, trying to move her lips. With no one to watch and listen, Siân would whisper to the photograph as though it were Faraway who had come to keep her company.

"Sarah Jane . . . Sarah Jane . . . I wonder where you are now. I wonder why you were so unhappy and afraid. If only you could speak to me."

Then, in her imagination, she would run her fingers through the girl's hair or touch her cheek and feel a tear there. If ever she had a sister of her own, it was Sarah Jane she would have chosen.

That night a veil of cloud hid the moon and Siân heard the raindrops pattering against her window. The wind freshened and began moaning under the eaves. For a long time she lay awake listening to its murmuring. Sometimes it sounded like an owl crying from its perch on a high bough, sometimes like a stream rushing down the hillside. And the more intently she listened the wilder became her thoughts. Then it was a prolonged sighing, now a voice in the distance, calling, calling.

The night wore on. But each time she drifted into sleep she was awakened by the constant tapping on her window and the sorrowful cry of the wind. Then came the darkest hour before the dawn.

It was not fear that made her heart leap as she sat up in bed. Sarah Jane had come to her from far away. It was her voice that sighed and beckoned. Into Siân's mind flashed images of seafarers sailing among the islands of the Aegean Sea. She understood how they were lured by the Sirens to the rocky shores, for there was she, like a moth drawn by a candle flame, leaving her room and wandering along the corridor. The lamp cast a pool of light around her, and with each step the calling seemed nearer.

Like a sleepwalker Siân descended the stairs until she was at the door of the little room below. She could not remember unfastening the bolt and going inside. It was not until she was halfway down the steps leading to the cellar that she became aware of her surroundings.

The wind stopped sighing. It was cold. There was no sound except an occasional drip of water falling from the walls into the shallow pool in the corner. The alcoves and farther corners were plunged in darkness. Broken barrels still lay sprawled upon the floor, and a beam hung loose from the ceiling. Siân shivered and pulled her nightdress tight about her chest.

"Where am I?" she whispered to herself, as though she had awakened from a dream. And then louder, into the dungeon below the steps: "Sarah Jane? Were you calling, Sarah Jane?"

There was no answer. Step by step she ventured down, watching, listening.

The lamp was trembling as she clutched the handrail and climbed back to the top. There she pulled hard to fasten the latch, passed by the brooms and pails, and emerged once more into the recess under the stairs.

She was surprised to find that it was morning already. Daylight was showing in the window above the front door and spilling into the corridor from the kitchen at the far end.

Siân looked about, bewildered. She remembered lying in bed listening to the rain pattering against her window and the sough of the wind. But then the sky was dark, with many hours to pass before daylight came. She wondered first if the clouds had drifted away and it was moonlight that came slanting in. Then the light grew brighter and a ray of sunshine appeared.

Each morning Frances and Emily rose early, but there

was no sign of anyone downstairs: no sound from the kitchen of the fire being laid or the clatter of breakfast dishes. Because she was a little afraid, that old shadow of loneliness crept over her. But there was one who had not forsaken her and appeared there at her side.

"It's so quiet!" whispered Faraway. "Where has everyone gone?"

They walked together toward the kitchen. The door to the lounge was open and Siân peeped inside. She gasped with astonishment. "It's all so different!"

The walls were bare, with none of the pictures in their gilt frames portraying the steamships upon the ocean, galleons with their guns ablaze, sailing vessels tossed by wind and waves—none of the scenes she remembered. There was no sign of the piano which had accompanied their singing on Christmas Eve, no grandfather clock standing in the corner.

With Faraway at her side she looked around in amazement. As if by some magic spell everything had changed. Where soft armchairs had stood upon the rugs around the fireplace, there was a long table with a scrubbed top and upright chairs scattered about. The floor, too, was bare, its boards scratched and dirty. Along the far end, almost hidden in the shadows, stood a counter upon which could be seen an assortment of bottles and a barrel similar in size to those that lay broken on the cellar floor.

A startling revelation awaited her in the kitchen. She recognized none of the furniture where only the evening before she had sat down to her supper and where Frances and Emily had been baking bread. The window that looked out over the back garden was smaller and set higher in the wall so that only treetops were visible.

"Look!" whispered Faraway, and Siân could feel his fingers clutching hers. "There's someone standing at the fire!"

It was a woman they saw there. Her face was hidden as she leaned forward to stir the logs, but she wore a long black dress and a bonnet covered her hair, just like the woman described in Sarah Jane's diary.

"Miss Jessica!" Siân cried, backing out of sight.

She wondered whether the old man's words had come true: that when the door above the cellar steps had been opened after being hidden for so many years past memories had somehow escaped, rising from the depths like mist drifting in the valley. Faraway stifled a cry and ran back along the corridor.

Quite unaware of Siân's presence, the woman turned from the hearth and came toward her. She was tall and lean with sharp features, but her eyes looked straight ahead as she approached the doorway. Miss Jessica passed through as though no one were there. After all, Siân reasoned, why should the woman notice someone who was just a ghost from the years to come? For now, wandering about the rooms of Crud-yr-Awel as it was long ago, it was she who was haunting the time when Miss Jessica lived there. Whether Siân had journeyed back through the years in a dream or by some vagary of time remained a mystery.

She watched the woman in black go to the foot of the stairs and climb to the second floor. She made no sound as she moved along. There was no rustle of her dress as she passed close by: no footfalls along the corridor and upon the stairs.

Once more Siân felt Faraway tugging at the sleeve of

her nightdress. "She moves silently, like a ghost!" he whispered.

"It's Miss Jessica!" Siân murmured to herself. "And if Miss Jessica has come then Sarah Jane can't be far away!"

With this thought to urge her on, she followed the woman up the stairs. But there was no sign of her on the second floor. Several of the doors were open, showing the inside of the rooms to be quite different from what they were only the night before. Gone were the pictures that hung from the walls in the captain's room; gone too was the chest of memories that usually stood in the corner. Instead the room was sparsely furnished with an old-fashioned bed strewn with blankets, a wicker chair, and a washstand upon which stood a china basin and ewer. A similar scene appeared before her in each room she explored. Everything familiar to her had mysteriously changed.

Sometimes she closed her eyes for a moment and then opened them again, expecting the visions to vanish.

"It's all so strange!" said Faraway, staring all about.

From the bottom of the flight of stairs which led to the attic, Siân caught sight of the woman again. She was standing outside the room where Siân had spent her first nights at Crud-yr-Awel. Then the woman was seen knocking at the door, but there was no sound as her knuckles rapped several times. Her lips moved as though she were calling to someone, but no voice was heard. Everything was eerily silent, like the pictures of a magic lantern.

Presently the door opened and a girl appeared there. Although she looked younger than the likeness on her photograph, there was no mistaking the sallow complexion and big, dark eyes.

"It *is* Sarah Jane!" exclaimed Siân, wondering at the whim of time that had brought the girl back again.

As though she had awakened from sleep, Sarah Jane rubbed her eyes and followed Miss Jessica down the stairs. They passed so close to Siân that she could have stretched out her fingers and touched them. But they did not glance her way. The woman retraced her steps along the corridor to rouse others from their beds—visitors, perhaps, who had spent the night at Crud-yr-Awel and would now continue on their journey.

She knocked first on the door of one of the guest rooms and then on the door of the room where Frances and Emily usually slept. Siân did not expect the sisters to answer, for everyone and everything that had once been familiar would now be lost in the future. Close by was the room next to the attic stairs where Siân had lain awake listening to the wind and rain. Could it have been only an hour ago when she left her bed to answer a distant call?

Now the door was closed and she could only imagine what she might find inside. This was the place, she remembered, where Sarah Jane was forbidden to enter and which she had described in her diary.

"The DEVIL locks the door to keep me out," Siân recalled. "Only Miss Jessica goes in . . . some secret is hidden inside."

But as she watched, Sarah Jane threw open the door and entered the room without fear. The bed near the window was tall and wide with a frilled canopy supported by four carved posts. More surprising was the discovery that Sarah Jane was not alone in the room. Where Siân usually slept there was a lady sitting on the edge of the bed. With her pale face and dark hair she bore a striking resemblance to Sarah Jane, who now ran into the room and sat beside her.

Siân watched as the lady put her arm around the girl's shoulder and held her close. They were laughing and talking together happily, but although they were clearly seen no sound was heard. It was likely that the girl was with the mother who would someday go away forever: that the time of fear and sadness had yet to come.

"It's so unreal!" muttered Siân, wondering if the characters from an old story had come to her in a dream. Then she imagined the nightmare unfolding. Already the ghosts of the past had come stealing back—Miss Jessica . . . Sarah Jane . . . the mother for whose arms she longed.

Furtively she looked along the corridor, her eyes searching each doorway. She feared that somewhere the DEVIL would be waiting!

With no grandfather clock to chime the passing hours, Siân could not tell how long she wandered the corridors of Crud-yr-Awel, lost in some forgotten time. Everything she saw was different from what she had known, with only the whereabouts of rooms and stairways as she remembered them. In silence the ghosts from long ago moved about the house, passing her by without a glance.

Before long, bright daylight came streaming through the windows, and just as mysteriously as they had appeared, the visions began to fade away. Slowly, almost imperceptibly at first, shapes and colors about her took on their familiar form. She had no recollection of returning to her room, but that was where she now found herself, the blankets and bedspread on her bed thrown aside as she had left them, and a lamp still held in her hand.

In the window, blue skies were showing, to tell her that the clouds had drifted away and a brighter day had begun.

CHAPTER 14

Time and Time Again

It was not long afterward when someone was heard knocking on Siân's door. She made no sound but listened until the knocking came again, wondering who might be waiting outside. Would she open the door to find a woman dressed in long black clothes standing there? But then, she argued, Miss Jessica belonged to another time—a world of shadows and silence. And of this forgotten world she would be hesitant to tell a soul, for her story was too incredible to believe. They would say that she had been taken there in a dream or a flight of imagination.

"It's a beautiful morning. I thought you would want to be up and about in the sunshine." It was Emily's voice that accompanied the tapping on her door. "Siân?" she called again. "Are you awake?"

Siân opened the door, relieved to find a familiar face smiling at her. Hurriedly she washed and dressed and went downstairs to the kitchen.

Passing along the corridor she peeped into Captain Howard's room and noticed the pictures hanging from the walls and his chest of memories standing in the corner. Everything was just as it had always been, and yet in her heart she felt that no dream could have been so vivid: that somehow, while she slept, the events of long ago had come stealing through the years and were hiding only moments away.

From the lounge came the chiming of the grandfather clock. The family were finishing their breakfast and talked of the long winter passing and of how they welcomed the blue skies and warmth of spring.

While she ate, Siân looked from one to another. "The days are getting longer," she said. "Soon it will be summer, and then the leaves will fall and autumn will come again. Time is like a mountain stream forever flowing on." And then, searchingly, "Wouldn't it be strange . . .? I mean, whatever would I do if I were to wake early one morning to find that during the night Time had moved so swiftly forward or backward that everyone I knew had gone, and about the house everything had changed—the furniture standing around the rooms, the trees in the garden . . .?"

Emily smiled. "If I were you I should close my eyes and fall asleep again. Then when you wake your nightmare would have gone."

The others sat silently, deep in thought. Frances lowered her eyes as though she remembered many happenings beyond understanding. The old man's brow was furrowed, for he too was searching his memory to recall some tale he had encountered during his seafaring days.

"Sometimes there are mysteries that have no logical explanation," he began. "Long ago the skipper and all

hands of an American sailing ship disappeared and no
one ever discovered what happened to them.''

''A storm at sea,'' Siân suggested. ''Or perhaps the
calling of the Sirens lured them onto the rocks.''

The old man shook his head. ''They were sailing far
from the Aegean. And the ship did not founder; it was
only those on board who vanished. It's a mystery well
known to all sailors.''

Frances and Emily rose to clear the table, but Siân sat
enthralled, her chin cradled in her hands.

''It happened in the winter of 1872,'' the captain went
on. ''That was when an English ship sighted the *Marie
Celeste* adrift in the Atlantic Ocean. Midway between the
Azores and the coast of Portugal she was found, in calm
seas and broad daylight.''

''Perhaps the ship had struck a reef hidden beneath the
water,'' Siân interrupted.

''Although two of her sails had been torn away, the
hull was undamaged and there was no danger of her
sinking. Yet not a soul remained on board. For miles
around, the sea was searched, but no one was ever
found!''

''A ghost ship!'' breathed Siân. ''It could have drifted
there from some other time!'' She had visions of the
Marie Celeste forever sailing the seven seas, with only a
ghostly crew to steer her: sailors who had perished long
years ago.

''It was not a phantom vessel,'' the captain assured
her. ''She was a sturdy craft of wooden structure and
canvas sail. Later she was towed to harbor in Gibraltar,
but the whereabouts of the crew will always remain a
mystery.''

As his story ended, so the chiming of the clock rang out again, reminding Siân that it was not only an old sailing ship abandoned on the high seas that was shrouded in mystery. A dark secret also hung over Crud-yr-Awel, once the home of a gaunt woman dressed in black, a frightened girl, and some Devil who tormented her.

The day continued fair, with a high arch of blue sky and sunshine pouring down. In the afternoon Siân wandered alone in the garden; and there, in the scented air among the fresh greenery of springtime, she forgot for a while the vagaries of Time and the visions that had haunted her through the hours of darkness and early dawn.

She stooped low to stare into the newly laid flower beds as though she could hear the seeds stirring in the black earth, struggling to peep at the sunshine. Among the green shoots on the lawn she watched a clump of crocuses, their petals unfurling purple and gold. From the trees farther away came the fluting song of the birds. Her mind was so absorbed with the beginning of new life that thoughts of long ago faded away.

It was evening when David came again. They spent the last hours of daylight hard at work farther along the garden, cutting the dead wood from the roses, clearing brambles, and scything away the long tufts of grass.

"Here's where we shall plant young apple trees," said David when they had stopped to rest. "Then one day they'll grow tall and bear fruit, just like the orchard that was here in the old days."

He pointed toward the oak tree whose boughs were green with new foliage. "It will stretch as far as the boundary wall."

For a while Siân's eyes lingered there, where ivy crept across the ground and curled around its trunk, and memories of Sarah Jane came stealing back.

Dusk was falling when they followed the path around the house to the front gate. Siân was quiet as they walked along. For her the approach of nightfall brought a strange excitement. She wondered what new adventure the hours of darkness might bring: whether, in her dreams or by the siren calling of the wind, she would be lured back to a time she never knew.

"Is the cellar to be bricked up again?" asked David, as though he were reading her thoughts.

"Someday," she answered idly.

He chuckled to himself. "Miss Frances will be afraid to close her eyes at night now that the witches and demons can escape!"

Siân looked at him uncertainly, wondering if he would understand. "It's an eerie place!" she ventured. "And it's not witches that hide in the darkness."

It was then that she told him her story of how the wind and rain had beckoned and drawn her down the stairs and corridors with her lamp to light the way. She could not tell whether he believed her, because he listened silently as her story unfolded.

"It was more real than a dream," she went on. "And yet all about me was dusky and still. The house was just as I remembered, but everyone had gone and the furniture in each room I saw was strange—quite different from the Crud-yr-Awel I know."

She paused, looking over her shoulder at the house now standing dark against the sunset, just as it had stood for more than a hundred years.

"Sometimes, when I was a little boy," David recalled, "my grandfather would sit beside me and tell me a bedtime story. My eyes would close as I listened to his voice, and I would fall asleep before the story was over. But while I slept it would go on in my dreams. Sometimes the story would end happily, but other times I would wake up in fright.

Siân looked puzzled.

"It's likely your visions came to you in a dream," said David, "just like the end of Grandfather's story came to me."

He went on to explain how Siân had perhaps lain awake during the night, her thoughts filled with the mystery of a hidden cellar beneath the house, and the happenings of far-off days she had read about in an old diary. Then in her imagination, he argued, she had relived the story which was smoldering in her memory. Ghostly characters had returned from the past and crept into her dreams.

"But it was all so real!" Siân said again. "It's as though through all these years Time had stood still, buried in a tomb beneath the house—imprisoned in the darkness, waiting there, struggling to escape. And once the tomb was opened the spell was broken and moments of the past were stirred to life again like . . ." She moved her hands helplessly, searching for an explanation. "Like an old clock that had been wound again!"

Of one thing she was sure. It was in the cellar where memories were hidden, and now they had been set free.

They said good-bye at the gate. Siân watched until David was almost out of sight. Then she went toward the porch. The trees were still and the birds had gone to roost. In the gathering darkness she began to wonder once more what new mystery the night would bring.

After supper she sat in the lounge with the old seafarer, discussing the caprice of Time. She understood why the revolving of the earth brought light and darkness and why its journey around the sun changed winter to spring and summer. But why should Time forever move forward? And whatever happened to Time that has passed?

Siân watched the pendulum of the grandfather clock as it swung from side to side, measuring each second. Then she leaned forward in her chair and touched the old man's hand, looking directly into his eyes. "If this is a happy moment," she said, "then why can't we capture it and keep it for always?"

He sighed and said, "It will never be forgotten if it stays in our memory." And Siân fancied it was a tear he brushed from his cheek with the sleeve of his cardigan.

That night, before climbing the stairs to her room, she lit a candle and peeped down into the cellar. The flame shone only on the top of the steps. Beyond was pitch-black and silent. Despite all his travels and wisdom the old man could not tell where past time had gone. But if it lived on in memories then she was sure that some had been buried there in the darkness, and, while everyone slept, it stirred from its resting place and passed that way again. Quietly she closed the door and went to bed.

CHAPTER 15

"It's the Devil!"

That night, while she lay awake, Siân did not raise the lid of the little jewelry box and listen to the lullaby it played. Nor did she turn the pages of the diary and read the secret thoughts of Sarah Jane. Instead she closed her eyes and imagined summer had come, picturing the garden in full bloom and bathed in sunshine. She saw a lawn of emerald green surrounded by an array of color. At its corner stood the rockery, with the lily pond below reflecting the blue of the sky. There were arches of roses, purple garlands of wisteria clinging to the walls, and from the flower beds the seeds they had planted now blossomed—pansies, marigolds, snapdragons, and a host of scarlet poppies—each bed edged with clusters of forget-me-nots.

Her thoughts were filled with all the beauty of nature instead of dwelling on people from another time.

As the spring wore on she slept soundly at night, tired after hours of toil in the garden. David came each evening when his work at Maesgwyn was done, and together they set about their task of restoring the grounds of Crud-yr-Awel. Sometimes he brought the pony and cart laden with swaths of turf cut from the hillside. Occasionally Alun and Mair came along with him to help. Paths were relaid with crazy paving, bonfires burned old wood and tangles of ivy, rustic arches were built for the roses and honeysuckle. And when the evenings were fair the family would stay outdoors for hours on end to sit in the sunshine and admire the beauty of the garden.

"If the stables were still standing," Emily used to say, "I could imagine the squire and his lady driving off in a stately horse and carriage, with a coachman at the reins."

It was a time to enjoy the promise of summer—long days and boundless skies, a time to roam the hills or fish in a mountain stream. Already ramblers and climbers had broken their journey to spend the night in the guest rooms. And as the weeks passed by, old mysteries were forgotten. The door leading to the cellar had remained closed and whatever memories lay below the steps were shut up in the darkness.

Then one night early in the summer when everyone was asleep, black clouds swept over the hills. Siân was awakened by the distant rumble of thunder. A sudden wind rustled the curtains and in its sigh she imagined she heard a voice calling to her again. It came from somewhere deep within the house.

Old fears and excitement were rekindled. At first she was inclined to bury her head in the pillow until the voice died away, but some strange attraction compelled her to listen. Her heart was pounding as she threw aside the bedclothes and walked across the room, drawn inexorably like the sailor lured by a Siren's calling. Flashes of lightning lit her way along the corridor and down the stairs. And there the sound of the wind grew louder, as though the sea were rushing over rocks in an underground cavern. "I'm here . . . here," it seemed to say as she was drawn closer to the cellar.

"It's the voices of long ago that are calling. Perhaps the ghosts will come back again!" It was Faraway who was whispering beside her. It was always he who came to share her fears when she was alone.

With no lamp to guide her she groped her way to the door above the steps. And when she lifted the latch, an icy draft escaped. Siân shivered as it rose from the cellar and almost tore the door from her grasp. Then, for a while, all was silent again.

It was still dark when she emerged from the little room below the stairs. There had been no further calling: no sound from the tomb below. The gathering storm lit up the house for moments at a time, and then, just as suddenly, everywhere was plunged in darkness. It seemed that day and night followed in rapid succession with no twilight in between.

At the foot of the stairs she paused to listen and look along the corridor. From the lounge came a confusion of voices, some murmuring, some raised in laughter and song. At first only dim shapes could be seen in the dim light. Then a flash of lightning illuminated the room, and for an instant she glimpsed a crowd of people sitting around the long table. Others stood in groups at the counter, and clouds of gray smoke hung in the air. One voice was raised above the others.

"Jessie!" it called harshly, and then again: "Jessie, turn up the lamps!"

Footsteps came hurrying from the kitchen, and as Miss Jessica passed her in the doorway Siân hid in the shadows. Presently the lamps burned brightly and shone on the faces of those gathered in the room. There were young men and old, most in simple clothes—shirts with open neck and rolled-up sleeves, coarse trousers and working boots. And all the while the hubbub continued as they drank their mugs of ale.

"It's a tavern, just as old Joseph Poulson remembered!" Siân exclaimed under her breath, recalling the story David's grandfather had once told her. "Farmers and shepherds have come from all around. And perhaps travelers journeying by coach spend the night in the rooms upstairs."

If it truly were a tavern and not a dream, then since the thunderclouds had come rolling over the hills, more than fifty years had drifted away.

Whenever anyone came near or appeared to look toward her, Siân cowered in the doorway or drew back into the corridor out of sight. However, she was soon to discover that although their eyes glanced her way, no one saw her waiting there, and she was encouraged to venture farther into the room. Most of them talked and sang in their native language which she could not understand. Others argued noisily. But it was the tavern keeper—the man standing beside Miss Jessica in the lamplight—who captured her attention and set her heart pounding.

He was tall and unshaven, with coarse features and eyes that burned fiercely.

"Where've you been hiding?" she heard him snarl when he had drained his mug and thrown it down on the counter. He was glaring at the woman and swayed unsteadily as though he had been drinking since the evening began. "Never about when there's work to be done!"

With an oath he pushed her aside and staggered to another door at the far end of the room, flinging it open to show the vivid flashes in the sky. "One last drink for the road," he called out. "Better get home before the storm breaks." Then he refilled his mug from the barrel and poured drinks for others who gathered around the counter. Whereupon the laughter and bawdy singing continued.

Miss Jessica returned to the kitchen, unaware that Siân was following her. On the fire a pot was simmering. She bent over it and stirred the contents, muttering to herself like a witch at a caldron preparing some special brew. To this she added the greenish-brown fruits of a strange herb, glancing slyly over her shoulder as the broth bubbled and steamed. What remained of the plant—the branched stems of gray and spotted purple with small white flowers—she threw into the flames and watched them burn. Presently a little of the recipe was poured into a cup and taken away.

Along the corridor went the woman in black, and like a shadow she climbed the stairs, with the cup held in her hand. With no fear of her presence being noticed, Siân followed in her footsteps until they came to the room near the stairs leading to the attic. There the woman opened the door and Siân could see someone lying on the bed. It was Sarah Jane's mother who lay there, flushed and shivering with fever. Her eyes were heavy and she barely had enough strength to raise her head from the pillow.

"Come, I've brought you a little broth for your

supper.'' Miss Jessica helped her to sit up and put the cup to her lips. "It will cool your fever and help you to sleep. There, just a few sips more. Soon you will be well again.''

Afterward the invalid lay back and Miss Jessica watched her close her eyes and waited until she had fallen asleep. Then she moved stealthily to the door, turned the key in the lock, and went downstairs.

The tavern was now almost deserted. Farmers and shepherds were making their way home before the thunderclouds passed overhead, and as the last of them left, the tavern keeper shut the door behind them.

"Jessie!" he called again, and the woman came hurrying from the kitchen to begin her task of cleaning and preparing the tavern for another night of merrymaking. And while she worked, her companion sat sullenly at the table, his eyes burning more fiercely than ever.

"It's the Devil!" Siân trembled, sure now that it was he whom Sarah Jane feared so. Even though she knew he was just a ghost from another time and could never harm her, she was afraid to go nearer.

The Devil looked about the room, pursing his lips grimly. "One day it will all be mine and yours: the house, the tavern, the gold rings in her jewelry box—all ours! No more slaving from morning till night. Better for us when she's gone forever.''

"It's the hangman for thieves and murderers if we're caught," said the woman fearfully.

"Ah, but who will ever know?" he chuckled. "Folk will say she died of the fever. A poor widow, with no kin in the world. Only an orphan girl to grieve for her . . .''

Miss Jessica looked at him suspiciously. "No harm

must come to Sarah Jane,'' she said. "She knows nothing of our secret.''

He took another draft from his mug of ale and lowered his voice. "Can't keep her here,'' he muttered. "She's only a child, but she has sharp eyes.'' He chuckled again. "Someday she'll go away. Not a soul will suspect us. No one has seen you searching in the moonlight by the woodlands and hedge banks. No one knows the secret of the witch's poison.''

"The witch's poison!'' The words tumbled through Siân's thoughts as she remembered the recipe Miss Jessica had prepared in the kitchen, the cup she had held to her victim's lips. There was no telling how long they had been hatching their cunning plot. Even now Sarah Jane's mother could lie dying with no one to help her.

Suddenly they were disturbed by a girl's voice calling from upstairs. The woman was startled. "It's Sarah Jane!'' she said. "Perhaps the thunder has wakened her.''

The girl had come down from the attic with a candle to light her way and she was standing at the door of her mother's room trying to get in.

"I heard her calling to me!'' she cried. "But I can't open the door. Why is it always locked?''

In the candlelight Siân could see the tears welling in her eyes. Miss Jessica put her arm around Sarah Jane's shoulder and tried to lead her away. "Your mother must stay in bed until her fever has gone. Perhaps she'll be better tomorrow. Come now,'' she persuaded, "let us leave her rest for a while.''

"It's been days since I saw her,'' Sarah Jane sobbed. "Will she be well again soon? Will she, Miss Jessica?''

Siân wondered at their wickedness and cunning. Could he truly be the Devil and she a witch who had fallen under his spell? And more fearful was the thought of Sarah Jane being left alone, helpless in their clutches.

Once more a voice was heard calling from within the room. The girl broke free, struggling to open the door: but Miss Jessica pulled her away, her hand clasped over her mouth to stifle the girl's cries.

Just then heavy footsteps were heard climbing the stairs and Siân trembled with fright, for it was the Devil who came toward them, his eyes blazing, his lips curled in a fearful grimace. Angrily he seized the girl and dragged her along the corridor. The candlestick fell from her hand as she fought to escape, but he held her fast.

"There's one place where no one will hear your screaming!" he was heard to shout as they disappeared in the darkness.

Somehow Siân found the courage to follow them down the stairs, for she well knew the place where no one would hear the girl's cries. "Sarah Jane . . ." she called, "you will not be alone." And her voice seemed to echo through the house.

Her courage deserted her halfway down the stairs, where she clung to the banister rail, listening as the cellar door was bolted and the crying grew faint. Then the Devil's footsteps moved toward the tavern.

Lost in a place and time she could not understand, Siân was afraid to venture farther. The storm drew nearer, with lightning flashes momentarily turning night into day. There was no sign of Miss Jessica on the second floor. But as Siân wandered back along the corridor, another door opened and she was aware of someone standing there.

"I dreamed I heard footsteps and voices crying out." It was Frances who spoke to her from the doorway. "Heavens, child," she scolded, "you should be fast asleep in bed!"

CHAPTER 16

The Full Moon

"But things don't happen that way in dreams," Siân argued stubbornly. "They are never so vivid, with one incident following another like the chapters in a storybook or just as they do in real life."

She and David were strolling around the paths after their work in the garden was finished, and in the bright sunshine her fears had melted away.

"Dreams are all confused," she said, "changing from one scene to another. I saw the tavern as clear as day, with farmers and shepherds laughing and singing . . ."

"The tavern?" David frowned.

"Your grandfather remembers that years ago Crud-yr-Awel was not as it is today. People have come and gone, and for a time no one lived here at all. But when he was a young man the house was a place where folk came from miles around to drink ale after a thirsty day in the hills. It was a tavern then."

"But that was long before we were born!"

"It was more than fifty years ago," Siân agreed. "Don't you understand? That's why it's all so mysteri-

ous. I could never dream of people and places I have
never known. Dreams are like memories, recalling times
when you were happy or afraid. Sometimes when I am
asleep I go back to the days when I was alone in the city
with nowhere to call my home. And when I wake I am so
happy to open the curtains and look out at the morning
light and the green hills rolling away in the distance. And
sometimes . . .'' She hesitated, lowering her eyes.
''Sometimes I dream we are together high on a mountain
path, looking down through wisps of cloud drifting over
banks of purple heather. And then when I wake
. . . Well, then I close my eyes again and wish I could
sleep on and on.''

''You see,'' David contended, ''it's not only memories
that dreams recall: not only people and places you know.
You have never been high on the mountain looking down
through the clouds. You have been there only in your
imagination. And it is your imagination and the memories
you have found in an old diary that take you back to the
time when Crud-yr-Awel was a tavern.''

Siân pondered for a while. ''Then who, save Sarah
Jane, would lure me to a place and a time I never knew?
And why is it from the cellar her voice always calls?
Sometimes I wonder if the house itself is alive, and down
there in the darkness its heart is beating.''

With her eyes bright and the words tumbling from her
lips, she went on to relate how, chapter by chapter, a
fearful story of long ago was unfolding: the story of some
Devil and a woman concocting a witch's brew, of the
locked room where the girl's mother lay dying, and of
Sarah Jane herself, forlorn and tormented.

''It's the Devil who locked her in the cellar,'' she

continued solemnly, "and his woman who searched the woodlands for the witch's brew."

"The Devil?" wondered David.

"I don't know his name, nor how he came to be there, but he is the drunken tavern keeper with an evil face and eyes that burn like fire. 'One day,' I heard him say, 'it will all be mine and yours: the house, the tavern, the gold rings in her jewelry box.' I wonder whatever became of him and his woman," she muttered absently. "Perhaps it was the hangman who put an end to their days of wickedness, just as the woman feared."

It was not the eyes of the Devil but Siân's imagination that burned like fire, thought David, as they leaned against the garden wall. "If the place is really haunted," he said, "there is no telling whose voice is calling from the cellar. It could be someone from the far distant past— not fifty years ago but more than a thousand!"

"Who?" Siân challenged. "A thousand years ago it was just a barren hill where Crud-yr-Awel now stands."

David closed his eyes and, with his brow furrowed, searched his imagination for a likely story.

"Perhaps one day," he said at last, "long ago in ancient times, the Celts and the Romans fought a battle on the hillside. Many men were slain and their bodies buried together in a cairn, with a mound of stones built there to mark their resting place."

"A cairn?" asked Siân.

"It is like a graveyard," David explained, "but instead of tombstones with epitaphs carved on them, stones were gathered from the hills and piled high in the shape of a pyramid. Then everyone would remember where the bones of warriors lay. The remains of cairns are sometimes found in the hills even though they were built more than a thousand years ago.''

He pondered for a while longer and then continued his story, watching the spark of interest in Siân's eyes.

''Perhaps a young man had lost his life in battle, and every day his sweetheart came to the burial mound to grieve for him.'' He looked at Siân with feigned solemnity. ''Would you mourn for me if I were slain in combat and buried under a rock in the mountain?''

She smiled and brushed away a lock of hair that had fallen over her forehead. ''If you were a Celtic warrior who had fallen in battle and our love was true I would lie upon the rock and die of a broken heart.''

''And so it came about with this maiden of years gone by,'' David went on. ''All day long she would stay at the graveside crying bitterly. She couldn't live without him and died there of a broken heart. After a time her bones were found among the stones of the mound. But her ghost would never leave the hillside.''

''What has that to do with the haunting of Crud-yr-Awel?'' Siân chided.

''But that's not the end of the story. Centuries passed by, and in time the cairn was lost when a road was made and a tavern was built where the warriors had been buried. But the ghost of the broken hearted maiden remained to haunt the tavern. Many a night, when all was still, the cries of battle returned and her voice was heard weeping in the cellar and calling the name of her loved one.''

Siân blinked her eyes slowly. ''That's only a story you've made up,'' she chided again. ''There was no noise of battle. The haunting sound in the cellar is like the

Sirens' call that lured sailors to the rocky shores, and soon afterward the house was filled with laughter and singing, raised voices and the cries of Sarah Jane . . . Frances heard it too,'' she remembered suddenly, ''because she was roused from her sleep and came to the door of her room. Isn't it strange?'' she added thoughtfully, as though the realization had only then occurred to her. ''There is just the sighing of the wind before the cellar door is opened. It is when a light shines down into the darkness that the past escapes. Then the house falls under a mysterious spell and ghosts appear.''

It seemed that nothing David could say would dissuade her. He shrugged and said, ''I think that sometimes you wander off into another world—a Wonderland of demons and witches. And if I don't hold you close, one day you will stay there forever.''

He sighed and led the way along the path toward the house.

''If you wait until dark,'' Siân said eagerly, ''we can open the cellar door and shine a light down into the darkness. Then perhaps the spell will be cast and we will travel to that Othertime together.''

There was fresh bread and oatcakes waiting for them in the kitchen. And while they ate they talked of their plans for the garden and of a journey to Mynydd Du (the Black Mountain) which David had long promised. For a time devils, witches, and the disquieting memories that escape from the cellar were forgotten.

Twilight came. It was when they were walking along the corridor to the front door that their thoughts turned again to the events of years gone by. The hallway was

filled with the scent of garlic, and they noticed that
freshly cut sprigs of its green leaves and white flowers
hung all about.

"Isn't it odd," said Siân, "that if voices and visions
come only in dreams the same dream came to haunt
Frances last night?"

David ventured inside the little room under the stairs
and opened the door at the entrance to the cellar. Siân
was behind him, peering over his shoulder. A faint shaft
of light fell on the top of the steps. Below was dark and
silent.

"I hear no wind sighing," he said scornfully. "No
voices calling."

He lit the candle which was kept on the shelf beside
them and then descended almost to the bottom. "You
see, there is no Devil with burning eyes: no girl hiding in
the corner. It is only the shadow of the banister that
moves across the floor."

Warily Siân followed, glancing back at each step,
afraid that the door might close and trap them inside. And
as she watched, the candle flickered and went out.

She scrambled up the steps and groped for the box of
matches on the shelf. But although she struck one after
another, holding them until the flames burned her fingers,
she saw no one in the cellar below her.

"David?" she called over and over, each time more
anxiously. But there was no answer.

In her confusion she wondered if he had climbed up
from the depths of the cellar while she was searching for
the matches, and was now waiting for her in the corridor.
She looked outside. And there a more startling surprise
awaited her.

She was aware of stealthy movements around her. The walls seemed to shimmer, and when all was clear again shapes and colors had changed. The twilight had turned to day and the house was strangely silent. The front door stood wide open, letting in bright sunlight and the sound of birds singing in the garden. She did not call to David again, for she knew he was now far away—in another place, another time.

It was a garden she had never seen before, and yet its appearance was vaguely familiar. A paved path wound its way through the trees to the back of the house. Even as she watched, a horse-drawn carriage appeared at the gate and came clattering along, with the coachman pulling on the reins. Several passengers alighted and made their way to the front door. They took no notice of the girl who stood at the doorway, nor did they walk around her. Instead they strode straight ahead, talking one with another, and passed right through her as though she were not there. And Siân could not but wonder whether they were ghosts in her time or she a ghost in theirs. The coachman flicked the reins and drove on.

It was a woman wearing a long black dress and poke bonnet who came to greet them. There was no mistaking the sharp features and piercing eyes of Miss Jessica.

"Come in," she said humbly. "You must be tired and thirsty after a long journey."

Siân had no wish to return to the tavern or anywhere within the house where the Devil might be waiting, so she made her way out into the garden, following the sound of the horse and carriage which had passed out of sight behind the trees.

The ground on either side of the path was overgrown

with a tangle of shrubbery. Briars and brambles spread their tentacles far and high so that it was difficult to see beyond them. She came eventually to a stable where the horses were unbridled and led inside, leaving the carriage resting on its shafts. The boundary walls had changed little with the passing years, their gray stones covered with ivy. There was no lawn with flower beds around its edge, and where the woodshed usually stood was now a barren patch where only thistles grew.

In the afternoon sunshine Siân wandered farther through her strange surroundings. And it was there, at the far end of the garden, where once again she came upon the girl who was so often in her thoughts. It was Sarah Jane who was strolling in the long grass under the apple trees.

She did not look around as Siân approached, but walked on under the overhanging boughs until at length she passed out of sight.

The afternoon lingered on, and Siân began to wonder whether she would have to wait until night before she found herself in the time where she belonged. It was usually during the hours of darkness when she returned from her strange journeys—and never far from the cellar, she recalled.

The breeze freshened when the sun went down and she retraced her steps to the house. The front door was still open and the murmur of voices now drifted out from the tavern. She was climbing the steps to the doorway when a creaking sound overhead prompted her to look up. What she discovered there brought a gasp of surprise to her lips.

A sign hanging above the door was swaying from side

to side in the wind. It showed the silhouette of rolling hills and, above them, a picture of a full moon shining in the sky.

"The Full Moon!" Siân breathed. And she recited from memory the words written in the pages of Sarah Jane's diary. ". . . and if I should ever go away forever, then search for me under the full moon . . . that's where I shall be waiting."

Before long Siân had returned to the cellar door and was once more peering down into the darkness.

"David?" she called. "David, where are you?"

She heard a shuffling on the steps below and David's voice answering her.

"Strike a match," he said in a half-frightened whisper. "I can't see in the dark."

She lit another match and in its glow saw him standing there, as though the candle he had carried down into the cellar had gone out only a moment ago.

CHAPTER 17

Mynydd Du

David climbed the steps and had barely crossed the threshold when Siân hurriedly closed the cellar door and fastened the bolt. She took his hand, holding it tightly as she led him out into the corridor.

"I thought you were lost and that I might never see you again," she said, tears welling in her eyes.

"Lost!" David exclaimed. "It was dark only for a moment when the candle went out."

He felt her hand trembling, and her face was ashen.

"That was more than an hour ago," she sobbed. "Many times I lit a match and called your name, but you did not answer and I could see no one on the steps."

Patiently he listened to her story in which she told of her wandering in the garden and finding herself in strange surroundings among sounds and visions of some other time: of travelers in a horse-drawn carriage, of Sarah Jane appearing under the trees. "And hanging above the door," she vowed, looking into his eyes, begging him to believe, "hanging there I saw a sign. It showed a full moon shining in the sky. Don't you remember? 'Search for me under the full moon.' That's what was written in the girl's diary. In olden days, when simple folk had not learned how to read, there were no names written on taverns. Instead they hung signs outside, with pictures painted on them.''

''A strange garden? A sign hanging from a tavern wall?'' David repeated suspiciously. ''And it was not twilight, but the middle of the day with the sun shining?''

''It had the same shape as our garden,'' Siân persisted, ''with ivy-covered walls all around. But it had been neglected and was overgrown with brambles and bushes.'' She wiped a tear from her cheek. ''And if they were just daydreams why should I remember them so vividly?''

It was later that evening when David left Crud-yr-Awel. Although Siân was distressed, he could not believe the fantasy of Time leaping backward and forward from one century to another while only moments passed. But he was troubled to see her so pale and afraid.

He took her to the lounge where usually a fire was lit after sundown, and there he sat with her beside the hearth.

''You see,'' he smiled, looking around the room, ''there are no farmers and shepherds laughing and singing: no wicked tavern keeper with burning eyes. Everything is as it should be.''

With the fire glowing and everyone gathered around to keep her company, Siân's fears were gradually fading away. It was little wonder she looked so wan, Emily had chided, for her thoughts forever dwelt on times that were gone and forgotten. She brought a hot drink from the kitchen and laid another log on the fire. ''Dreams and memories,'' she muttered. ''Whatever will you imagine next!'' Then she smiled and ruffled Siân's hair affectionately.

"The years that have gone will never return," said the old sea captain, "so it is never wise to dwell on the past. Memories are what we treasure when we are old. And no one knows what fortunes the future holds. Better to be happy while you are young, for someday they are the memories you will recall."

Siân sighed, trying as best she knew how to understand the old man's philosophy. "Sometimes memories bring nightmares," she said at last.

"Now that summer is here," he went on, "you should spend more time away from this gloomy old house—walking in the hills, fishing in the streams. The sunshine and clean mountain air will put the jewels back in your eyes."

David responded eagerly. "We could climb Mynydd Du," he said. "Then you will truly be able to look down on drifts of cloud and banks of heather."

And all the while Frances sat silently, wondering perhaps if Siân too was gifted with the "second sight" and could experience happenings beyond the understanding of others.

It was early the following morning when David came again. He left his pony tethered at the gate while Siân prepared for their journey to the Black Mountain. She wore her stout shoes and packed a rucksack with food to last them through the day. There had been no overnight guests to accommodate at Crud-yr-Awel, so they were able to make an early start.

The sun had risen above the hills when they reached the bridge, and from high in the saddle Siân could see its rays reflected in the water like silvery flames. It seemed a long time since she had climbed to the other side of the valley, picking her way among the snowdrifts. Now the path was clear, fringed with gorse and fronds of ferns, and the distant bleating of sheep told her that Maesgwyn was not far away.

For a time they stayed at the farm, where Jess was unsaddled and turned loose to graze. There were many friends to greet her, first among them being Shep and Nell who came bounding over the hillside in answer to David's whistle. Mair brought a woolly lamb cradled in her arms, and little Annie told of a rocking horse that had stood alone in an attic for a long time. "Mummy thinks we should call him Dapple because he has patches all over," she said excitedly. "And he's not alone anymore. Every day we gallop over the mountains, and when he is tired he rests beside my bed."

Alun and his father were already out on the hills, and David's mother was frying eggs and bacon over the fire, insisting that they should not set off on their journey before breakfast.

"Sut ydych chi, fy ngeneth? [How are you, my young lady?]" It was old Joseph Poulson who called to Siân from his chair near the fireplace. "The girl from Tŷ-yn-y-Cysgodian—the House in the Shadows," he smiled.

"It's not so shadowy as you remember, Dadcu," said David. "We have cut away the old wood and brambles and planted flower beds and built arches of roses all along the paths."

After friendly words of welcome and smiles of admiration for one so fair, he invited Siân to sit beside him.

Then he puffed at his pipe and began reminiscing on the old days.

"It was not the trees that cast the shadows," he remembered. "They say it was the dark deeds that went on behind the shutters."

"That was a long time ago," she ventured, "when the house was a tavern and the garden was overgrown. The Full Moon it was called. Do you remember the sign hanging over the door—a picture of hills and a black sky above with the moon as bright as a sovereign?"

The old man shook his head. "The Full Moon? I can't recall its name. Tŷ-yn-y-Cysgodian, that's what folk hereabouts called the place. It was always . . ."

"Was there a red sky last night, Dadcu?" David interrupted when he noticed that faraway look in Siân's eyes. "We are going to climb to the first ridge of Mynydd Du and wonder if the view will be clear."

"There will be no cloud in summer while the wind is from the east," his grandfather forecast. "Every good shepherd knows that." Then he fell to reminiscing once more. "Yes, it was always a strange house, fy ngeneth. No one ever knew . . ."

"We shall have to start soon," David broke in again. "It is a long walk to the mountain and we must be back before nightfall."

When breakfast was over they set off to the north, pausing at the brow of the hill to wave to the children. Soon Maesgwyn had fallen out of sight and the mountains towered on the horizon. They walked on over dales and hills that rolled like waves in an angry sea, through woodland and along a riverbank. And the farther they traveled the higher grew the mountains before them. Siân gazed in wonder, for no building she had ever seen in the city stood so majestically against the sky.

Before they began to ascend the slopes of Mynydd Du, they stopped to drink at a mountain stream and look at the beauty around them.

"If Time is like a river," mused Siân, "flowing on forever and ever, there must be a beginning and an end. The river is fed by the streams and ends its journey at the sea."

"Then from the seas the wind gathers moisture and clouds are formed," David explained. "And from the clouds rain falls on the mountains and the journey begins all over again. So the river flows on forever."

"But where does Time begin and end?" Siân wondered. "How old are the mountains, and where did they come from?"

David searched his memory to recall what once he had learned at school. Having lived all his life in the shadow of the mountains he had often wondered that himself.

"They have been there almost since the beginning of time," he remembered. "Hundreds of millions of years ago when the earth was taking shape. Continents moved and volcanoes burst from the center of the earth, and from great oceans the mountains rose."

"Mountains rose from the sea!" Siân looked at him incredulously.

"Scientists know this is true," David argued. "Bedded among the rocks on the mountaintops they have found countless fossils and shells of creatures that once lived in the sea."

"Perhaps that is why the hills rise and fall gently like the waves," Siân suggested.

"The hills are not nearly as old as the rocky mountains. Millions of years later the earth was gripped in an ice age. Then, when the glaciers melted and moved across the land, hills and valleys took shape."

In Siân's imagination a million years was an eternity— a measure beyond her understanding. And in the realms of Time, happenings of just fifty years ago were truly only moments away.

"Why," she said, "perhaps it was only yesterday when the Cradle of the Winds—when the House in the Shadows, as your grandfather remembers it—had a picture of the full moon hanging over its door!"

The slopes of Mynydd Du were steep and rocky. David led the way, choosing the easier paths and sometimes taking his companion's hand to help her along. At frequent intervals they stopped to rest and look down on the hills and valleys that stretched below them. They saw an undulating patchwork of green, with darker woodland and silver threads where rivers wound in the distance. Siân imagined herself as a mariner of long ago, aloft in the rigging, looking upon the heaving waves, and then as an eagle, watching from its aerie the silent world beneath. If they had stood there a million years ago, she thought, they would have perished in a caldron of fiery lava. Now there were only rocks and tufts of bracken on the shoulder of Mynydd Du.

Their journey to the ridge was long and tiring, and there they stayed for an hour or more until the sun began to fall in the sky. David pointed out the peaks of Snowdon, and farther to the south lay the distant shores of Cardigan Bay. Above them stretched a fathomless ocean of blue.

"It's so peaceful," Siân sighed. "If it were not so far I would come here every day."

"The mountains can be treacherous," David warned. "Sometimes clouds close in around you and there would be no landmarks to show the way home. You should never climb the mountains alone—not even on a summer's day."

For a while Siân was quiet, wondering if she should disclose a secret she had shared with no one: afraid that David might laugh at her strange reverie. "I would not always be alone," she faltered. "Whenever I am lonely or frightened Faraway comes to keep me company."

"Faraway?"

"I know he lives only in my imagination, but sometimes he is as real to me as any boy might be. Long ago he came to me in a dream and never went away. I call him Faraway because that's where he came from. Now I see him only faintly and he never stays long."

"Perhaps that's because you are no longer lonely and afraid," David smiled with understanding. "Anyway, if ever you are lost in the mountains and Faraway has gone, then I will come to rescue you."

"It's just a foolish fancy," said Siân. "Promise you will never tell." Her deep blue eyes met David's. "Now that I have a true friend perhaps he will go away for always."

Their rucksacks were lighter when they left the ridge and picked their way down the mountain paths. They had eaten the food they carried and now wore their cardigans against the chill of late afternoon. It had been a day Siân would always remember—a time she wished would never pass as the river flowing on.

CHAPTER 18

The Gravediggers

It was early in the evening when they returned to Crud-yr-Awel, but twilight lingered for several hours. Before supper David and Siân strolled in the garden, planning other journeys not far away.

"There are the Swallow Falls across the Conwy River," David suggested. "and nearby are the ruins of an old Roman fort."

"We could wait there until moonlight and perhaps hear the ghostly sounds of Celtic warriors in battle," Siân teased.

"And to the east is Mynydd Hiraethog, with dense woods covering the lower slopes." David lowered his voice. "They say that witches gather there at Halloween."

For miles around, the countryside was rich with places of interest and beauty. They talked of lakes and mountains, of Clocaenog Forest and the legendary Beddgelert (Grave of Gelert) farther to the west and east.

But on that summer evening, and for many days to come, there was no mention of the tavern in that Othertime or the cellar from which memories escaped.

David hoped that this would be forgotten and that never again would Siân fall under its spell. In the days that followed, its door remained bolted and she had promised that if ever the wind sighed during the night and she imagined a voice calling to her, she would bury her head in the pillow until she had fallen asleep again.

They were not to know then that her next visit to the Full Moon would bring visions more vivid and happenings more fearful than ever before.

It all began one morning that summer when Siân came upon the little jewelry box in the cupboard of her room. The beads and trinkets that someone had put there years ago were still hidden inside, together with some of the rare stones Captain Howard had gathered from the night markets of the East and had given to her as a keepsake. She turned the winder underneath and as the lullaby began to play, old memories were awakened.

The tune rang out clearly in the hollow of her room. It drifted out into the corridor and down the stairs where Emily's voice was heard singing the words. "Breichiau mam sy'n dyn am danat" [Mother's arms are folding round you]. And as the singing continued, Siân realized with a start that it was not Emily she heard but the voice of a girl. It reverberated through the house, seeming one moment to come from the attic and the next from somewhere downstairs. When the jewelry box was closed the singing ceased, only to return immediately the lid was raised again. It had happened more than once before, she remembered: while she was alone with Faraway, searching among the jumble in the attic, then again on Christmas Eve when the lullaby was played on the piano and Frances's eyes had strayed to the door.

As the music box played on she went outside her room, listening first at the foot of the stairs below the attic and then over the banister at the other end of the corridor. Yet the girl's voice was all about her, like echoes in a cave.

She was surprised to discover that the door in the recess below the stairs was wide open and that the ray of a flashlight was moving around inside. It was the old sea captain she found searching around in the darkness.

"You heard it too?" Siân questioned. "Someone singing that sad lullaby?"

"Someone singing?" he said absently. "No, my love, I have just been looking down into the cellar which you and Frances find so mysterious. I wonder why it has been bricked up all these years?"

"Perhaps it holds frightful memories—" Siân suggested, "hides some secret which is best forgotten."

The steps were steep, and the old man trod carefully as he descended them, flashing his light all around. "It's so deep and cold. I wonder what it was used for?"

Siân shuddered. "It could have been used as a dungeon to keep someone prisoner. But David's grandfather remembers that when he was a young man Crud-yr-Awel was a tavern. Then it would have been a cool place to store the barrels of ale. You see the broken hoops and staves lying on the floor?"

"A musty, miserable place," the old man muttered. "Better that its dark secrets be sealed up again and forgotten."

And so he resolved that before autumn came the door at the entrance should once more be hidden with brick and plaster, never again to be found.

He turned off his flashlight, leaving the cellar in

pitch-darkness, and Siân heard him climbing the steps more hurriedly than he had gone down. She held the door open, waiting for him to appear.

It was then that the voice of Sarah Jane returned, on this occasion not singing a lullaby but crying pitifully.

"Don't leave me here," she sobbed, "it's so cold and dark!"

The old man had not heard her cries, for his footsteps did not falter. Even when a scream rang out from the cellar, he did not switch on his flashlight to see who was there.

When he emerged into the daylight at the top of the steps, Siân stood back, frozen with terror. It was not the face of Captain Howard she saw, but the cruel grimace and burning eyes of the tavern keeper.

"The more you shout and scream the longer you'll stay there!" the Devil called down fiercely. Then, after shutting the door and sliding the bolt, he strode off into the corridor muttering oaths, and the girl's crying grew faint.

As she stole from the shadowy recess, Siân stared, wide-eyed, at the scene that confronted her. The stairway and the walls about her shimmered like the surface of water ruffled by the wind. Shapes and colors were swiftly and silently transformed until the house she knew took on a new dimension. The long table with groups of strangers sitting around and the drone of their voices told her that the lounge had become a tavern again. The tavern keeper was among them, his raucous voice raised above all others.

Although no one would have seen her or known of her presence there, Siân was afraid to venture inside. Instead

she returned to the place where Sarah Jane was imprisoned and listened at the cellar door. She heard the girl's
fists beating upon it and her cries pleading to be let out.
Many times Siân called her name and struggled to release
the bolt, but her voice was not heard and her fingers were
like shadows clutching at the door. For a long time she
stayed there, desperate to set the captive free, yet
powerless to do so.

It seemed that hours passed before the noise from the
tavern subsided. Some who had been drinking there
staggered along the corridor on their way to the front
door, pausing to listen near the cellar, thinking that they
heard someone cry out.

"It's only the old crone calling from upstairs," said
one. "Jessica, the witch," laughed another. "Her voice
sounds softer after a mug or two of ale."

When the house became silent, Sarah Jane's cries were
more clearly heard. "You can't keep me here forever,"
she sobbed. "I'll . . . I'll run away. Then everyone will
know . . ." A moment later the pounding began again.

And as the girl wept and beat upon the door, footsteps
approached. It was the tavern keeper—the Devil
himself—who strode from the tavern, his lips twisted
with rage. Close behind him came Miss Jessica.

"Someone will hear her," she whispered, looking all
about.

The Devil carried a lamp, and when the cellar door was
flung open, Sarah Jane shielded her eyes from the glare of
its light.

"Run away, would you!" he snarled. "That's if ever
you have the chance."

Angrily he pushed her down into the darkness. She

screamed as she stumbled and fell to the bottom of the steps where she lay quite still.

"There's no one to hear you now," he muttered as he bent over her, tying a gag tightly over her mouth with the kerchief he took from around his neck. "And here you will stay, cold and hungry, until you learn to do as you're told!"

Miss Jessica peered down from the top of the steps. "She's not moving," she said. "God help us if any harm should come to her. The hangman will get you for sure!"

"Then it is you who will stand beside me on the gallows," came the Devil's sullen reply. "Remember who searched the woods and marshes for the witch's poison that sent her mother to her grave!"

Once more the cellar door was bolted and the girl was left lying where she fell. Siân held her breath as the murderous tavern keeper and his woman came close. But they passed her by without a sidelong glance, and she heaved a sigh when she heard their footsteps going up the stairs.

As she had feared, each event recorded in Sarah Jane's diary was unfolding with stark reality. Her mother had gone, slowly poisoned by the deadly hemlock gathered from the marshes, and left to suffer behind the locked door of her room. Miss Jessica . . . the Devil . . . the cold, dark dungeon where Sarah Jane was held captive. It had all come true, with only one grisly chapter unfulfilled. The words burned in Siân's memory. ". . . and if I should go away forever then search for me under the full moon . . . that's where I shall be waiting." And the prospect of Sarah Jane never escaping from the cellar filled her with horror.

She listened at the door. There was no more crying: no sound from within. Many times she called the girl's name, softly at first and then at the top of her voice, remembering that no one would hear her—not even Sarah Jane she realized at last. There was nothing she could do but wait until the nightmare passed.

Sometime later the sound of footsteps came again, growing louder as they descended the stairs. And there, framed in the glow of their lamp, the tavern keeper and his woman appeared. They paused for a moment, leaning over the banister rail to listen.

"It's quiet now," Miss Jessica whispered. "Open the door and let her out," she urged. "She can do no harm. She's only a girl. Who would believe her wild stories?"

The Devil's lips were set grimly. His eyes smoldered.

At length they unbolted the door and went down into the cellar. Siân watched from the top of the steps. The girl still lay sprawled where she had fallen. They took the lamp close and untied the gag from her mouth. There was blood smeared on her forehead and a fixed stare in her eyes which remained even when the glare of the light fell on her face. One arm hung limp across her body, the other lay twisted at her side.

The woman stifled a cry. "You've killed her!" she said, wringing her hands anxiously. "There's nothing can save us now!"

Siân turned away in horror. Her worst fears had been realized. "Sarah Jane! . . . NO, it can't be true!" she cried, covering her eyes, longing that her nightmare would go away: that the visions would grow faint and vanish.

When she looked again, the Devil was standing over

the girl's body. "Struck her head when she fell," he muttered. But the woman thought it likely that she had suffocated with the kerchief bound tightly around her face.

"Now our secret will be safe," he grinned. "She can never tell her story to a soul."

Furtively, Jessica raised her eyes to the open door above the steps. And for a moment Siân's heart leaped when she imagined that her presence had been discovered.

"We must bury her in the marshes," said the woman, satisfied that no one was watching at the cellar door. "Far from the house where she'll not be found. We'll say she ran away and vowed never to come back again."

The Devil scowled. "It's a long way to the marshes at Coed-y-Celyn. Safer to bury her here. There's no one but you and me who ever set foot in the cellar."

He took the girl's hands and dragged her body to the darkest corner while his accomplice hurried away to find a make-shift shroud and something with which to dig the grave.

Presently she returned with fire irons from the tavern and a blanket draped over her arm. And there, in a secluded alcove, by the glow of their lamp, their heinous task began.

The body was wrapped in the blanket and when the flagstones had been raised, a shallow grave was dug in the earth.

For a long time the silence in the cellar was broken only by the sounds of their labored breathing and the digging away of earth and stones.

"No one will find her there," the Devil declared,

picking up the lamp and searching around for any tell-tale signs of their sinister deed.

Once more Siân hid in the shadows as she heard them climbing the steps. Then a silhouette emerged from the cellar doorway.

"Yes, my love, a musty, miserable place. Better that its dark secrets be sealed up again and forgotten."

It was the voice of Captain Howard she heard, as though he were repeating what he had said only moments before.

CHAPTER 19

"*Is Anyone There?*"

The old man could see the fear in Siân's eyes. He put his arm around her shoulder and led her into the daylight. "We'll take a stroll in the garden," he said. "There's nothing like the sunshine to drive away your troubles."

And there, among the trees and flowers, with the scent of honeysuckle in the air, the color returned to her cheeks and she felt that at last she had awakened from her nightmare.

"It's over now," she told him. "No more wandering: no more daydreams. It's like coming to the last page of a storybook."

They were walking slowly along the path under the trellised arches, and Siân took the old man's arm to help him along. He reached up to pick a rose and put it in her hair.

"Sometimes it's sad when a story comes to an end," he said. "But they are usually spun in someone's imagination. They are not real like a bright summer morning or golden hair and eyes as blue as the sky."

He looked into her face, smiling. Then they stopped to

rest on a rustic seat which David had made from fallen boughs gathered in the woods.

Siân took the rose from her hair and touched its petals idly. "Some are true, even though it's hard to believe them. Remember the ghost island of Pulau Hantu where the warriors fought over buried treasure?"

"A tale of mystery," he recalled, "perhaps with a grain of truth and much imagination, embellished each time it is told."

"And the ghostly tales of the sea—the Sirens who lured sailors to the rocky shores, the *Marie Celeste*, the murdered girl whose ghost appeared on the deck of an Irish mail boat? Were they only imagined?"

The old man pondered for a moment. "Ghostly tales are the most mysterious, and no one can ever tell for sure if they are true."

Siân brushed the rose petals against her cheek, her eyes wandering to the farthest end of the garden. "I don't think anyone will believe me," she began, "but I know that ghosts linger in this house. Cradle of the Winds . . . House in the Shadows . . . the Full Moon . . . Whatever its name might be it hides an awful secret and has a fearful story to tell. In my dreams . . . in my imagination . . . each chapter unfolds like the pictures in a storybook, and now the story is at an end."

The old man sat quietly as she recalled each of her journeys into that Othertime. She told of the lonely Sarah Jane who grieved for her lost mother, of witch's brew, of the tavern keeper and his woman who tormented the girl. At first there had been only footsteps and murmuring voices. Then after the cellar had been discovered, each time its door was opened the haunting became more vivid. It was surely from the cellar where frightful memories escaped.

"Isn't it said," asked Siân, "that ghosts always return to the place where they lived and died? The warriors of Pulau Hantu came back to fight for their buried treasure. The ghost of a woman returned to the ship where she had met her death. And now," she added gravely, "Sarah Jane calls from the place where she lies buried. Unless her spirit finds peace she will haunt the house forever."

The old man rose from the seat. It was a comfort to learn that Siân's nightmares—her journeys into the past—were over. "Before the long nights come again," he promised once more, "the cellar and all the memories it holds will be sealed up, perhaps until the house falls to ruin. Then you can dream of happier times waiting in the future."

Uneasily Siân followed him along the path. "But Sarah Jane will never go away. She will haunt the house and garden until . . ." She turned to look again toward the boundary wall where an orchard once grew. "She will never go until her ghost is laid to rest."

As he had promised, that evening Captain Howard made arrangements for the entrance to the cellar to be covered up again. Some time within the next few days David was to take his pony and cart to a merchant in the village for the materials needed to rebuild the wall.

Although it was dusk, Siân was reluctant to go indoors and had stayed in the garden all day long, fearful of venturing near the foot of the stairs.

"It's like a mystery story coming true," she said when she and David were alone. "Each chapter unfolding just as it is written in Sarah Jane's diary. And now the story has ended.''

David sighed. ''No more daydreams, no more tears. All those memories will be hidden in the past where they belong.''

But Siân knew that the last frightful memory could never be forgotten. '' '. . . if I should go away forever, then search for me under the full moon . . .' '' she murmured to herself. ''Remember how we searched for her grave in the churchyard? It's under the tavern where she will be waiting. That's where she was buried.''

''If there ever was a tavern, a witch who gathered deadly herbs, a Devil with burning eyes . . . If ever they lived here at Crud-yr-Awel then now they are dead and gone!''

''Sarah Jane will never go away,'' Siân answered gravely. ''Her spirit will find no rest.''

''But when the cellar is hidden,'' said David, ''she will stay there in the darkness, and there will be no voices calling to you.''

If Sarah Jane's body truly lay buried in a shallow grave beneath the house, then it was soon to be discovered that her ghost lingered on.

That evening David went alone to the cellar. He took a flashlight to examine the crumbling wall he was to rebuild. Jagged brickwork framed the door which was now closed and bolted. Fresh sprigs of garlic were strewn upon the floor and hung from the latch, suspended by a knot of red ribbon. He smiled at Frances's time-worn spells and wondered if she shared Siân's daydreams.

When he opened the door and shone the flashlight down into the gloomy alcoves, the foretelling written long ago crept into his thoughts. It was here where they should search for a forlorn girl who had gone away forever.

Slowly he descended the steps, leaning over the rail to explore the hidden corners with the beam of his flashlight. The broken barrels still lay sprawled on the flagstones, and drips of water fell intermittently from the walls. He stopped before he reached the bottom of the steps, watching, listening. As the light moved from corner to corner, shadows scurried across the floor like clouds passing over the face of the moon. And for the first time he felt strangely uneasy, as though he were intruding in some forbidden sanctuary.

The door above creaked on its hinges, suggesting that someone had stolen past him on the steps and was escaping unnoticed, or else someone were creeping in and moving down the steps behind him. He looked up, calling in little more than a whisper. "Siân . . .?"

He thought perhaps she had followed him there. But there was no answer.

"Is anyone there?"

The cellar was silent, except for the occasional dripping of the water. Then there came sounds which made his heart beat faster. There was a grating, as of flagstones being dragged one upon another, a scratching and scraping of earth as though someone were digging a grave, the sound of feet shuffling about, and the unmistakable rhythm of breathing. Yet as the ray of the flashlight moved across the floor, from the foot of the steps to the farthest alcove, nothing in the cellar stirred. Minutes passed before there was a further sound of flagstones being moved and replaced upon the earth. Then for a while all was silent again.

More frightening was the voice that came reverberating through the cellar. It was singing the same sad lullaby he remembered from his childhood and which many times Siân had listened to on the music box. "Breichiau mam sy'n dyn am danat [Mother's arms are folding round you]." It seemed to come from somewhere far away and echo there in the darkness.

Before it had faded away he hurried to the top of the steps, closing the door behind him.

It was almost dark when David left Crud-yr-Awel and stood on the brow of the hill which led down into the valley, looking back at the house now showing black against the skyline. In his thoughts another voice echoed. "Sarah Jane will never go away," Siân had said. "Her spirit will find no rest."

At last he began to realize that it was not just her imagination that conjured sounds and visions: that her journeys to that Othertime were not daydreams. He knew now as surely as night follows day. When they uncovered a doorway which had been hidden for more than fifty years, they had disturbed memories which should have lain buried for always.

CHAPTER 20

"She Is Gone Forever"

After the startling events of the day neither Siân nor David could rest peacefully that night. For hours they tossed and turned in their beds, their imaginations running wild. Their fitful sleep brought dreams of mysterious sounds and of lurid visions which haunted the cellar. They both longed for daylight when they would be together again. And early the following morning David returned to Crud-yr-Awel where Siân had waited anxiously.

"It's the gravediggers you heard," she told him when he recalled the sounds that frightened him away. "And it was the voice of Sarah Jane that echoed there."

She told how she had heard the singing whenever the lullaby was played, but then she thought it had been only Frances and Faraway who heard it too. Now she knew it was not her imagination and that if, as she feared, Sarah Jane was buried in the cellar, then her remains would be lying there still.

"Isn't it strange," Siân wondered, "why some can look into the unknown while others see nothing at all?

163

Sometimes I see things happening in my dreams as clearly as when I am awake.''

David seemed to understand. "Perhaps ghosts appear only to those who want to believe," he said.

Later that morning they replenished the firesides with logs from the woodshed, and as they walked to and from the house Siân's thoughts were far away.

"Often I feel she is watching when I wander in the garden. I hear her in the attic, and once she appeared as clear as day standing under the oak tree." Siân sighed. "Her ghost will linger here for always. If only . . ."

"If only her resting place were found!" David interrupted suddenly. "Then perhaps she would be seen and heard no more." He shrugged helplessly. "But we could search the cellar floor for days and days and never find her grave."

Siân trembled at the thought of rummaging in that dark and awesome tomb where the Devil and his woman might dwell, her gaunt form and his fiery eyes appearing there in the shadows. She imagined that as they searched in the lamplight the door would shut fast above them and a constant wind would wail, smothering their cries.

"I would not be so afraid if you were there beside me," she said bravely.

Frances and Emily were preparing the guest rooms and their father was engrossed with his model of the eighteenth-century sailing ship when David and Siân came in from the garden and ventured once more beyond the cellar door.

David led the way down the steps, treading gingerly in the pools of light cast by the lamp. Siân followed, clutching at his sleeve. Her eyes searched below, and each moment she expected the shadows to transform into the long black gown of Miss Jessica.

"It's there I saw them," she whispered, pointing to the farthest alcove.

She held the lamp while David dislodged the flagstones and dragged them aside. Then, with the spade he had brought from the woodshed, he began to dig into the earth beneath, pausing at intervals to listen for the ghostly sounds he had heard when he was alone there.

Deeper and deeper he dug, until a mound was piled beside them and water seeped into the cavity.

"It was a long time ago," he muttered. "Perhaps we are searching in the wrong place. Perhaps they were sounds we just imagined," he added miserably.

He rested for a while and then removed the flagstones lying against the wall nearby; and there their search continued.

Presently the spade struck an obstruction a foot or so beneath the surface. They held the lamp close and gazed in horror at what they discovered there. Among shreds of rotted material lay the disjointed bones of a skeleton. And as the light fell upon the gruesome remains, the cellar became bitterly cold.

Siân's lips trembled. She was too numbed to cry out, and the lamp fell from her grasp.

In the darkness David led her away, groping for the handrail and scrambling to the top of the steps. Before they reached the doorway they heard furtive movements behind them—a scratching and scraping upon the floor, the dragging of flagstones—as though the gravediggers had returned.

                          *   *   *

A stunned silence fell upon the house when their discovery was revealed. Emily stared in disbelief. Frances wrung her hands nervously, wandering around from room to room, all the time muttering to herself. It was only Captain Howard who accompanied David to look into the shallow grave.

Now he understood why the cellar had remained hidden through the years: why everyone was forbidden to enter. It was either the murderers who had thrown a cloak over their crime or later inhabitants of Crud-yr-Awel who had built a wall concealing the door so that ghostly sounds could not escape. And now the secret was uncovered. Frances's foreboding . . . Siân's daydreams . . . her journeys into another time . . . now they all seemed more real.

The discovery was reported to the village constable; and in the days that followed, many official visitors called at the house, each investigating the sinister happenings of years ago. But there was little light anyone could shed on the mystery. The captain explained how the hidden door had been found by chance behind the crumbling wall. The whereabouts of those who had lived there in the past were unknown, and even when some were later traced they could offer no explanation. They told of ghostly sounds that were sometimes heard in the downstairs corridor and described the house as cold and eerie.

It was the story told by David and Siân which the county inspector found most curious. He peered over the rim of his spectacles. "Sarah Jane?" he frowned. "Well now, young lady, isn't it strange that you should know the name of someone who lived here so long ago? And stranger still that you should find the place where she lay buried?''

Siân looked at him anxiously, wondering if he would believe her story.

''Among some playthings in the attic I found a little book,'' she began. ''Inside Sarah Jane had written her secret thoughts . . .''

''Secret thoughts?'' the inspector repeated thoughtfully.

''She longed for her mother who had gone away, and told of a Devil who locked her in the cellar and left her there, alone and afraid.'' Siân hesitated, fighting back the tears that welled in her eyes. ''There was no one to help her. Often I . . . dreamed that the house crept back to that time long ago, and I was there with her. Sometimes . . . in my dreams . . . I saw the garden and the tavern as it used to be. David's grandfather remembers that when he was a young man the house was a tavern for shepherds and farmers,'' she explained hurriedly, seeing the puzzled look on his face. ''But the Devil was always there . . . always watching her!''

She described the wicked tavern keeper, a woman in a black gown, the crying in the cellar, the sounds and visions that came in her dreams. The inspector raised his eyebrows, but listened patiently.

''At first no one would believe her story,'' David told him. But when he had gone into the cellar he had heard the same strange sounds that Siân described and knew that he was not alone there. ''Something was moving in the darkness,'' he explained. ''There were footsteps shuffling around and the sound of someone digging in the earth.''

The investigation continued throughout the day. The little book in which Sarah Jane had recorded some of the happenings of years ago was examined and taken away. In the cellar no stone was left unturned. But Time had drawn a dark veil over the mystery and now the truth would never be uncovered.

The summer wore on. Although a wall now hid the cellar door again and it was only the wind that sometimes sighed in the corridors of Crud-yr-Awel, memories of Sarah Jane lingered on.

From the garden Siân watched the evening sunlight filter through the trees and glisten on the windows of the house, while David swept the first fallen leaves from the path.

"She is gone forever," she said sadly. "She will never come back again. Perhaps she is at rest now that she is buried in the churchyard."

David looked at her and smiled. "No more daydreams and nightmares to call you away." He leaned on the broom, thinking aloud. "I wonder whatever happened to the tavern keeper and his woman? The wicked will never find rest, my dadcu always says."

"They may have cheated the hangman," Siân sighed, "but they would have been haunted until their dying day."

Retribution would be sure, she imagined, for the fearful memories that sometimes escaped from the cellar would have remained forever in their hearts and thoughts—calling, tormenting, whether they were awake or asleep. They might even pursue them beyond the grave.

It was arranged that David should stay that night at Crud-yr-Awel, for the next day they were to explore the eastern slopes of Mynydd Du before the mists of autumn came, and they were to set off on their journey at first light.

Somehow the house seemed brighter now that the cloud of mystery had drifted away. The last rays of the sun came slanting through the windows and the evening passed peaccfully.

It was when supper was over that the old voyager took David and Siân to his room, proudly to display the model of the eighteenth-century three-master, with the sails unfurled and its name carved upon the hull.

"The *Moonflower!*" Siân whispered in admiration. "It is more graceful than any ship that sailed the seas."

"Sadly my seafaring days are over," the old man said. "It is for you to keep and to bring good fortune as you embark on your voyage through life." He took it from the table and placed it in her hands. "Perhaps someday you will journey to the ghost island of Pulau Hantu and find the warriors' gold and jewels buried there."

"Or listen to the Sirens calling from the rocky shores of the Aegean Sea." Siân smiled and kissed his cheek. "I will treasure it always."

It was early in the morning when they set off for the mountains. As they passed through the village they broke their journey to visit a lonely grave in the corner of the churchyard. The mound of earth was smothered with forget-me-nots and they looked sadly at the epitaph carved on the headstone. "Sarah Jane. Rest in Peace," it read simply. And underneath was written the beginning of a lullaby she used to sing.

They recited the words together. "Breichiau mam sy'n
dyn am danat—Mother's arms are folding round you."
Then David took Siân's hand and led her away, and for
the last time she imagined she heard Sarah Jane's voice
echoing in the hills.

Postscript

Although the characters and incident in the foregoing story are imagined, the folklore of North Wales tells of a tavern near the border between the old counties of Denbigh and Caernarvon which provided overnight shelter for travelers journeying from England to Ireland during the nineteenth century.

It is remembered as a dark, forbidding place, the haunt of thieves and highwaymen. It stood on the edge of woodland somewhere along the road from Cerrig-y-Drudion (Rocks of the Daring One) and Betws-y-Coed (Prayer House in the Wood) at a time when the highway was a rough road for horse and carriage.

So fearful was its history that its reputation as a house of evil and mystery spread throughout the neighboring counties, and only the unwary ever darkened its doorway.

Accounts of the strange happenings there appear in an anthology of tales about North Wales; and the tavern is featured in the novel *House in the Shadows*, both by the Author.